Praise for *On a LARP*

"A fast-paced whirlwind ride that dives into the fascinating world of Live Action Role Playing. Sid Rubin is one of those brilliant and smart heroines you would happily follow even to the darkest parts of the Web . . . Deoul has brought an incredibly fun and fresh voice to the YA genre."

—Ileen Maisel,
Executive Producer, *The Golden Compass*

"It's all very high concept, this stream-of-consciousness monologue that takes place in a split second as our young protagonist falls to her certain death. And yet, it not only works, it works magnificently—mostly because Deoul has taken complete control of her young heroine's voice. Sid is the smartest seventeen-year old you've never met, at once funny and brilliant, forthright and insecure, too-good-to-be-true and utterly real. Once you have met her, you won't forget her soon."

—Eric Peterson, *NBC OUT*

"Twists and turns abound in Stefani Deoul's fast-paced fun new book. With a clever and sharp heroine, find a comfy chair . . . You will be there awhile reading this terrific debut."

—Lee Rose, WGA Nominee,
The Truth About Jane;
Humanitas Prize Finalist,
A Mother's Prayer

Praise for *On a LARP*

"Upon reading the first pages of *On a LARP*, I felt as if I'd been grabbed by the scruff of the neck and lifted from the ordinary world into a parallel reality fueled by fast action, cracked neurons, and foul play. Accomplished author Stefani Deoul introduces Sid Rubin, a smartass—and actually super smart—high school kid with a strong conscience and a knack for solving problems. Of course, problems aren't hard to come by in Sid's life, especially dangerous ones. Sharp readers will appreciate this steampunk'd, high-tech'd tale."

—Elizabeth Sims,
Lambda Literary Award winner, *Damn Straight*

"If you like your high adventure flying down the information superhighway, and are craving a cracking murder mystery, look no further than Stefani Deoul's infectious caper, On a LARP. Sid Rubin is a new kind of hero— way too smart and just a little too sarcastic. Deoul manages to inject Sid with the perfect degree of high school stream of consciousness, where every thought can run in ten directions, and yet find its way back to the original source at just the right moment . . . most of the time. Sid and her friends are characters you care about, and this adventure is full of all the danger, young love, intense passions, and self-doubt that make teenage life today so extraordinary."

—Shamim Sarif, Writer, Producer, and
Director of the Award-winning books and films,
The World Unseen, I Can't Think Straight
and *Despite the Falling Snow*

On a LARP

A Sid Rubin Silicon Alley Adventure

Stefani Deoul

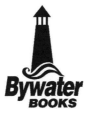

Ann Arbor
2017

Bywater Books

Print ISBN: 978-1-61294-095-3

Bywater Books First Edition: April 2017

Printed in the United States of America on acid-free paper.

Cover designer: TreeHouse Studio, Winston-Salem, NC

E-Book ISBN: 978-1-61294-096-0

Bywater Books
PO Box 3671
Ann Arbor MI 48106-3671
www.bywaterbooks.com

For 14

Love 16

Possible worlds are a fantastic matrix.

—Victor Hugo*

* As read on the internet . . .

. . . which we know makes it true.

PROLOGUE

Pop quiz! Only one question.

Do any of you know the truly scary part about being seventeen?

Okay. Time's up.

Let's check your answers.

If you guessed a) first romantic love, you would be annoying, slightly behind the curve, and . . . wrong. For those of you who went with b) driving without parent . . . wrong again.

Now, if you actually gambled on c) "love is meant for beauty queens," etc., you would be not only so, *so* wrong, but you also just publicly pleaded guilty to the charge of listening to your parents' music. You are now sentenced to the wearing of your very own, personal Scarlet "L." Hawthorne fans everywhere shall rise and rejoice. But clearly I digress. Which is something I should admit up front I have a rather amazing, if somewhat dubious, talent for.

And while I am sure there will be more on this as we mosey along, for now let us return to the question at hand. Which was, "what is the truly scary part of being seventeen?" And no, the answer is not d) everything and it is also not the cheap trick of answers e) all of the above.

The correct answer is—drumroll please—you still have an impossibly, unbelievably, underdeveloped brain. And yes, I am not making this up.

According to a study I read on the internet, by the National Institute of Mental Health, the brain is not fully developed until a person is—get this!—in his or her twenties. The parts of the brain that control emotional and impulsive behavior have not yet

1

matured in teens, and "such a changing balance might provide clues to a youthful appetite for novelty, and a tendency to act on impulse-without regard for the risk."

Helloooo? Stay with me people.

Fine. I will cut to the chase and give you . . . the critical part:

As the frontal lobe is one of the last parts of the brain to develop, and IN THE TEENAGE BRAIN, IT'S NOT REALLY FIRING AT ALL, it is therefore physiologically harder for a teen to completely understand the future consequences of his (or her— as this case may be) emotional or impulsive actions. Some psychologist named Laurence Steinberg once compared this lack of teenage brain phenomena (in a manner I am now applauding as both succinct and accurate) to "a car with a good accelerator but a weak brake."

I personally like to think of myself as a mint-condition 1966 Mustang. Convertible. Cherry Red. Digression.

So back to my point, in simple English, all this means is your teenage brain doesn't know, understand or care what it can't do; and while this sounds great in theory, in practice it honestly is not always such a good thing.

In my particular case, my underdeveloped brain apparently didn't know I couldn't fly.

So I jumped . . .

And I plummeted . . .

And I promise you, if I somehow manage to survive this act of immature-brain-encased-in-unbelievable-stupidity, I will gladly tell you exactly how I got here . . .

. . . Ah yes, well, here.

I guess one might be wondering where exactly here would be. Well, I am, as my Aunt Megan would say, "in Rat City wearing cheese pants." I don't know why she says that or where

2

that particular expression comes from but I love it. And it is a brilliant summation of my current dilemma.

However, for those of you seeking an answer with perhaps a bit more specificity, "here" is above the marble floor of Astor Hall, inside the Main Entrance to the New York Public Library, soaring through the air, flailing wildly downward.

And for those of you who might not be familiar with this particular library, before you climb the steps to gain entry to this imposing tomb of tomes (witty, no?), you stride right between the two fierce lions standing watch over this castle.

Their names are actually Leo Astor and Leo Lenox. They were named for the library's founders, were designed by Edward Clark Potter and carved by the same guys who carved Abraham Lincoln sitting in his memorial in Washington, DC. But sometime in the 1930s Mayor LaGuardia nicknamed them Patience and Fortitude. Which kind of stuck.

And it is this insightful educational moment, which brings me to my current rather loose, free-floating brain cell query. If I'd been thinking about Patience and Fortitude and sticking around, rather than rushing off to play hero, would I have ignored what could have been a lifesaving portent, and thus averted finding myself trapped, or perhaps more accurately, suspended, in this predicament? I'd like to imagine I would, but in all honesty it most likely would not have deterred yours truly.

And you want to know something else, something *truly* freaky? It is absolutely amazing how much stuff can flit through your brain while you are plunging to your death.

It is an absolute paradox. I mean, think about it. Intellectually we can agree the laws of physics demand that I be dropping like a rock and yet this free fall is one gigantic run-on sentence. It is a lesson in massive stream of consciousness, tumbling run-on thoughts of useless minutia—all while simultaneously experiencing a white-noise, shrieking train of thought: *How can I possibly have enough time to be thinking all of this?*

So the room below is spinning and there I am flying somewhere the heck over what I thought should be the epicenter, which was where I calculated *he* ought to be, holding his gun, when I note that spot is empty. Yet as we have discussed, my mind keeps churning with irreverent tangents, even as the floor grows closer, neither my eyes nor brain willing to acknowledge that I could have missed him.

After all, I do not miss the dude with the clarinet—random, I know! His dyed red hair spiffed into an impossible pompadour, his bow tie covered with some cool gear pattern, hanging starchly untied (letting me know it's for looks only), staring up at me with ever-widening eyes and a kind of smirk—all while not missing a beat. This I am managing to register and even be dimly aware he is playing something kind of familiar. But whatever tune it might be is drowned out by a new insistent interloper.

"Recalculating. Recalculating." Really! Suddenly cutting through the competing voices of my mind, I hear her specific voice—at once shrill, demanding and demeaning—the GPS witch woman. OMG, I am going to die and all I can hear is Helga. I am trapped in a dashboard in my mind.

But then I do hear it. I know I hear it. It's a bang. A *big* bang. From somewhere over the ballroom lamp. But I can't see it. No muzzle flash. No smoke. Where is she? Where is he? It isn't making any sense. Where is the spiral of smoke? Why is there a red spot appearing below? The red spot is spreading. Almost like a bull's-eye forming just below me. Weird. Shouldn't there be a spiral of smoke? I hope my shoes don't get scuffed. I bought them just for tonight. They're very black and white, very old-school 1940s Spectators. So freaking perfect. I told myself to take a shoefie. I told myself, but I did not listen to myself. It will *so* suck if they get ruined.

You know my friends, the floor is rapidly approaching and I have just enough time left to be guessing this is a probably a consummate example of what Dad meant when he said I needed to learn to look before I leap. But now, it is so way too late for that, and worse, I still don't understand why I can't see it.

There's always a spiral of smoke in the movies.

4

ONE

I guess we should start at the beginning.

My name is Sid. Sid Rubin. Actually if I am going to be honest about it, my name is Sidonie, which no one is allowed to call me except my Mom and my grandmother. And they only get away with it because they're French. Yes, as in "From France." As in wine and *ma cherie* and brie cheese and croissants. Ooh La La.

My dad (Noah) met my mom (Juliette) when he was at an astrophysics conference in Europe. According to Dad, he was there to talk about the stars but after he saw Mom the only stars he could see were the ones in her eyes. Every time he tells this story, I snort. Dad also claims he wanted to name me Nebula so I should thank Mom every day for ignoring him and sticking with Sidonie. And although I will concede he has a valid point, I will also point out he was actually the first one to call me Sid, so honestly, I don't really think he likes Sidonie all that much, either.

I have a younger brother, Jean, whom I have to begrudgingly admit has it worse than me. At least I can go by Sid, if not voluntarily, at least defensively. Jean, on the other hand, is also meant to be French and if you were reading it, it would be pronounced kind of like ZHAN, but every year without fail, the teacher taking roll yells out Jean as in Gene like DNA or jean like blue jeans—one of which is the girl's name and one of which is short for Eugene—and neither of which bodes well for him. And so every year, just like it's all brand new all over again, the kids start calling him YOOOOO GENE or YOOOOO

HOOOO(blow a kiss) JEAN—depending entirely on just how moronic they are.

It is absofrickinglutely amazing how stupid just never seems to get old.

You would think by high school everyone would move on, but noooo, there he was, first day, freshman year, too short, too nerdy and slinking his way down the hall pretending he couldn't be bothered to answer the taunts. And sadly, Jean is not a name that lends itself to a cool nickname. So sometimes even I have to say, it really does suck being him. And I do think even Dad secretly agrees with this. He once said "It seemed like a good idea at the time," which given his usual bias means Mom got all French on him while saying this is what we should name our son and he just agreed. He never stopped to think about anything other than how Mom said it. In our house, the general rule is when Mom gets "all French," Mom wins.

By now I would hope I have gotten you to the feeling-sorry-enough-for-us stage but, just in case, one more tidbit to add to the growing pile. We're both reasonably classified as brainiacs. And therefore any last shred of hope of fitting in would be an abstract concept.

But I do possess one secret weapon. And it's not just any old secret weapon. My secret weapon is James "Jimmy" Flynn. Yep. Five Fingers Flynn. Six foot four and still growing possessed of an arm that can throw a ball nearly the full length of a football field and put it through the swinging tire at the far end. Yep. My best friend is Jimmy Flynn, star quarterback. And when your best friend is the star quarterback, you get high school immunity. The geeks are my friends because I am one of them, but all the other cliques who would gleefully kick me to the curb are always ever so slightly fake gushy as they seek to ingratiate themselves so they might worship at the Throne of The Flynn.

And while you might assume that being Jimmy Flynn is simple and glorifying, nothing about Jimmy Flynn is necessarily simple nor what one would expect. For starters, Jimmy's Dad is 100 percent Irish American, born and raised in Boston. His

Mom, however, is 100 percent Japanese American, born and raised in Charleston. He is also the star quarterback who is busy trying to decide whether or not he should attend Harvard, Yale, or Princeton. His other sport of choice is chess.

The Flynn's secret dream is to be a Supreme Court Justice. And when you know Jimmy it makes perfect sense—his ability to take in his world, analyze the information, and see how a choice will impact and resonate far beyond the moment we are in. Works in football, works in future judge world, and probably needless to say it is a quality I sorely lack.

Jimmy and I met at what I like to call one of those super-market sweepstake events for fast-tracking your self-proclaimed, uber-bright toddler into the right school. Our moms started chatting and the next thing you know we have our first play date. We were two. By the time we hit nursery school we were not only old pals, we were best buds.

I remember when SuSu Roberts, who at age four was already a fully committed *entitlementist*, swiped my crayons. Before my first indignant tear could shed, Jimmy came tearing across the room, walked over to SuSu and declared, "You are not being *behaved*. You give Sid back her crayons." Well, SuSu glared and stamped, even tossed her colorfully beaded hair, in an apparent attempt to rally a standoff in the pre-k corral, but Jimmy didn't move (come to think of it, neither did Mrs. Trebont) and so SuSu sucked in her cheeks and flounced herself around and handed them back. Then Jimmy yelled, "Say you're sorry." And she did. And after that, no one could pick on me. Jimmy Flynn had my back. And that was long before any of us knew he would be Five Fingers Flynn.

For me, the scariest part of thinking ahead to graduation is coming to terms with knowing I will have to find my own well of courage forward, without my personal knight to protect me. And why is that so scary? Maybe because even by high school it is obvious, in so many ways we never truly move beyond our pre-k universe.

TWO

So now that you've met the players, well at least the ones you needed to know to be up to speed, let's get down to how it all began.

There we were, thirteen of us, sitting in Mr. Clifton's AP class—Morality, Legality, and Life—intensely discussing a TED Talk Mr. Clifton had just made us watch. It's this concept by Derek Silvers and it's all about how to supposedly start a movement. It has a guy dancing around all crazy in this field—alone. And there are all these other people in the field just staring at him. Suddenly one guy joins him, and then everyone else gets up and they're all just dancing in this field.

Yeah, I know; I hear you. But it really was kind of interesting. And according to Derek Silvers, the second guy is the first follower and he is the one who transforms the guy from a lone nut to someone who's leading the way of something.

And judging by class pleaser Vikram Patel's effusive nodding, he is definitely seconding something or other Jimmy has just raised, and two things occur to me: one, I am so not listening, because two, from my vantage point in the far corner of our classroom couch I realize this whole concept is kind of a study in the engineering of Jimmy Flynn. He's one of those guys who effortlessly gets a first follower. And funny enough, that isn't me. I'm just his buddy. The first followers always just come because Jimmy says, "hey, here's a great idea," or some such thing. However, it is important for me to disclose in fairness, sometimes, I am a first benefiter—but that arrangement isn't in this particular TED talk.

So anyway, after Mr. Clifton had us watch this TED talk, we began loosely debating historical context for the talk. You know, take the biggies and theorize. Ready, set, go: Without a first follower, would Hitler have remained an ugly, hate-filled nutjob? And what about one of the supreme biggies, Jesus? Would Jesus have simply lived and loved and perhaps have been known as one of those sons who never leave home? Would all the neighbors have gossiped about what a disappointment he must be to his mother? Would that have been their stories were it not for their first followers?

And because Mr. Clifton epitomizes cool—and not just because he commutes on his personally restored motorcycle, one rare and sexy 1947 Indian Chief, has gauges in his ears and a mysterious tattoo running up his arm, but because his conversations are not those whereby the teacher writes on the blackboard and we raise our hands as a sign we wish to share—we are involved.

We, this chosen baker's dozen, are sitting, or more accurately practicing the art of couch slouch, in the "den" area Mr. Clifton has designed at the back of his classroom, complete with a series of mismatched sectional sofa pieces positioned to surround the conversational centerpiece, an oversized, funky coffee table, which is a sloganeer's delight, having been layered over and over again with stickers people have contributed—from peace signs and smiley faces to anti-this and pro-that and just about any cultural reference the Smithsonian could be looking to collect.

And while to the uninitiated this table might appear ready for its own reality series, *Decoupage Gone Bad Season 16*, each sticker has a story. Every student is required to find a sticker, bring it in, and earn a place on the table by arguing why their sticker is a necessary addition to this installation. It is, I kid you not, the class final. If your sticker does not make it onto the table, one third of your grade is an automatic F. With this sticker you must define what its message will contribute not only today, but tomorrow. And by extension, what will you?

And so while we sip on this cocktail of equal parts simplicity and complexity our uber-cool Mr. Clifton serves up, we do it from lattes we have whipped up in our single-serve, but yet eco-friendly and recyclable, coffee pods. And while we practice being ever so pseudo-adult by debating virtues and vices, theories and conspiracies, and of course, saving the world, we make it so much more earnest but still filled with savoir faire by munching multigrain lemon cranberry scones from the (of course) locally sourced corner bakery.

And as is par for the course (pun intended, people!), Mr. Clifton has once again not only successfully engaged our attention, but ratcheted it up to a full-blown conversation, which for most high school teachers would be victory enough. But not Mr. Clifton.

And thus we find ourselves relishing heading off to our local police station so we can meet with a sergeant and explore our newly devised theories about leaders and followers. Presumably we will also hear their thoughts about the practical implications of the talk, but it will require they cut through our nearly evangelical zeal. How many people are in lockup that perhaps would not have committed their offense were it not for finding a first follower? Would there be a Clyde without a Bonnie? How critical is that first follower person to a specific type of criminal? If there are lone wolf killers, are there specifically first follower bank robbers or killers? Is it profile-able?

And what about the psychology of the dude who stood up to start dancing second? What makes a first follower follow?

And if you really think about it, it is kind of interesting, because if you take someone like Charles Manson, he never actually did kill anyone, directly. But his followers did. So is he our prototype? If he were never able to gain a first follower, would Helter Skelter have happened? Could it?

Okay. So maybe you are not finding this quite as fascinating as I did. However, even my zeal of fascination is rapidly deflating as we stand here gathered in this overcrowded, old, and just kind of suffering from that not-so-fresh feeling (and I am referencing not only the building, but some of the clientele) station into which we have been surreally transported and sensory slapped.

Sometimes, you know, old is glorious; think burnished woods

and tarnished coppers. Sometimes old is, well, just kind of nasty. I think there's a color scheme that would best describe the spectrum of the palette decaying before our eyes, and I want to call it puce, but I know puce isn't right. Puce green is a falsity; puce is actually purplish brown. I think I mostly want it to be puce because it is so close to puke that it wants to be right. But it isn't. Whatever the color scheme, my body recoils.

But before we, or at least I, can think to beat a retreat, a sharply dressed woman greets Mr. Clifton, and with a round of hand-shaking our fates are sealed. We are given the signal to trudge our way into a group and, just as we begin the forward-ho shuffle, a uniformed cop leads what I can most fairly describe as an apparent homeless man right through the center of our assembled mass.

Let me be clear as I share with you, my friends, an important understanding here in as polite a manner as possible. I do not believe most people are homeless by choice. And I understand niceties we take for granted are not within their daily reach. However, in this moment, what I also know is this apparently homeless man has no access to personal hygiene products or opportunity. And because sometimes understatement is more revealing than effusiveness will ever be, I will leave you with a simple, sincere visual: the odor was not looking good.

And given the previously mentioned overall sickly hue in which we stood, I begin to find myself inching my way closer to The Flynn while trying not to actually touch anything and debating just how interesting this really is, and I'm kind of busy not making eye contact with anything. Which is how I came to trip over my own feet and nose plant into Jimmy's back, forcing an exhale of my breath which I had been holding, which in turn forced me to raise my nose out of Jimmy's back in order to inhale for a brief moment and, thus, is how I came to see *her.*

"To see who?" you wonder.

That is how I came to see Tessa Sargentino. I know it feels as though I should be saying how I came to meet her, but the truth is she was just a photograph on the wall of a room we were walking past. And because I looked up when I tripped and because I had seen that same photograph in the morning paper, I thought it a perfectly opportune time to nudge Flynn and point her out through the open door. Because my theory, which I had explained most enthusiastically to The Flynn earlier, was she had been to a LARP before she got killed.

And now, it was not only one, but a series of crime scene photos we could kind of, but not really, see through this partially open door, and along with the obvious tell-tale signs of murder (you know, a body impossibly skewed and lots of blood), I noticed the one from the morning news, the one in which she was wearing a striking and unusual outfit. Très Edwardian Mistress of the Steampunk. If she wasn't lying dead in the photos, I must admit, I might have felt a twinge of envy at what would have been her obvious, uhm, flair in that bustier.

So as I am pointing through the door to the photo and saying, "I'm telling you, it was a LARP. Check out the outfit." A rather bulky man gave a cursory "Ahem" while pushing right on by as though we weren't actually standing there, and then turns back to finish his interruption of me and Jimmy with what novelists like to call a "curious look," right before closing the door in our faces.

If perchance (isn't that just such a great word? I love when I can find a place to use a great word) you are wondering if I had some kind of portent about this meeting, I will let my next words speak for precisely how I felt in that moment. I looked at Jimmy and proclaimed, "Asshole." I also remembered the name for the puke color I was looking for is chartreuse. And that sums up just how deep I felt my first meeting with Detective Robert Tsarnowsky went.

THREE

Fast-forward seventy-two hours.

And here I am, hanging out at Perk This, the attitudinally challenged, weirdly velvet-draped coffee shop around the corner from our school, working on an SAT tutorial with Imani Cruz. Imani and I met when she transferred into our school right after her dad got transferred from his diplomatic job in the Netherlands to his new one at the UN. I was assigned to be her "friend" and show her around. At the time, she was a chubby, awkward frizzy-haired twelve-year-old and somehow the ever ubiquitous "they" decided I was apparently the best equipped to handle the job.

Not that I was chubby. For the record, I have never been chubby. Lanky. Not chubby. Lean. Maybe a wee bit on the string bean-y, flat-chested side of life. Maybe. And I can sort of concede I was awkward. And I wore really thick glasses. And yes, they were nerd glasses. And yes, they called me Velma. For some of us, finding a personal style isn't necessarily intuitive.

And while the powers that be were right about our hitting it off (or maybe they didn't actually give it any thought other than geek meet geek), they were really wrong about how it would all turn out. It wasn't that Imani wasn't smart. Her language skills are off the chart, an advantage of having been born in Kenya but "posted" to Japan, Germany, Spain, and the Netherlands. She actually speaks six languages fluently. But too many schools in too many countries does catch up with one, and Imani's deep, dark, safe-with-me secret is she really can't add two plus two and

15

get four. But I can. I can actually add two plus two and get answers most people can't even think up, never mind actualize. And it isn't like you need to be a math genius to study acting at a first-rate liberal arts school, but you still have to at least respectably pass, if not ace, the SAT.

Oh. And for the record, on that other score of geek meet geek? Imani grew seven inches in two years, allowed her amazingly white but rather buck teeth to be turned into a gorgeous and now metal-free smile, relaxed her frizz, and all of a sudden, in our senior year, all the boys (and yes, some of the girls) want to date our very own, capable of swearing in six languages, stunningly sexy and still charmingly accented Ms. Cruz. I, meanwhile, have learned that my very lean and lanky, boyishly charming, dark, brooding looks, offset with ultra-pale aquamarine eyes (which are still enhanced by square-ish, black frames, albeit mod ones—and the occasional Slytherin tie) and possessing a natural, very thin streak of oddly white hair, have a very nice and enigmatic place in this world. Thank you very much. And for the record, I now consider being called a Velma my highest compliment (hence my homage-laden eyewear). But then again, on the ceiling of my bedroom I have an enormous sign; it reads THE GEEK SHALL INHERIT THE EARTH. I like to dream on that one.

I know. I digress. So, where were we? That would be you and me.

Aha! We, that would be Imani and I, were sitting in the back corner of Perk This, my trying to explain a math equation from one of those "previously on SAT" books when behind my back the door opens and in saunters Jimmy Flynn, accompanied by the smirkiest of smirks. Something greasy this way comes.

As he arrives, I look up, take in the hands in his pocket, tongue kind of pushing into his cheek, rocking side-by-side fake nonchalance. "Yeah?"

Again his stupid smirk threatens to pop back out. I can just sense it tugging its way out from the corner of his mouth. "Um. Someone's looking for you."

What is he up to? That's my real question. But asking it would be too obvious, might even border on a bit desperate. I leave it tucked away so we may continue the game. "Yeah?"

I know. Scintillating. But before we can get into the next round of this incredibly deep exchange, someone comes up behind Jimmy. And my mouth quite simply drops open. And the world around me spins. And who knew that when my world spins, the dance track accompanying it would be The Laugh of The Flynn.

It was *her*. I mean it wasn't her, but it was. I found her by accident one rainy day, cruising playlists, watching movies online. Suddenly there she was and my world was rocked. It was an old film, made in 1987. I have now watched it approximately a zillion times and forced Jimmy Flynn to watch it at least half a zillion times. I have spent my entire teenage coming-of-age, hormone-induced fantasies torn between wanting to be Mary Stuart Masterson in *Some Kind of Wonderful*, or wanting to rescue Mary Stuart Masterson from *Some Kind of Wonderful*. And suddenly, here she was. My fantasy. Come to life. I mean she wasn't. But she was. It was her!

Blubber, blubber, yammer, stammer. Georgie Porgie Pudding and Pie.

OMG! If there was ever a question as to why my nickname is not and has never been Suave Sid, let us all rest assured this is what one might call a seminal moment complete with a revealing flourish of an answer. Never has and now we know for certain, never will be. I am a tower of babblement.

Wow. Heat. So freaking hot in here. Face burn. Face burn. Can't breathe. Need air. Who knew a person could not only hear, but actually feel, their heart pound in their ears? Pounding. Pounding. And as it pounds, it also shudders.

My impending cardiac arrest is mercifully interrupted by the sudden appearance of one forward-thrusting, large, ungainly, and yet bizarrely recognizable cop. This new juxtaposition of persons takes my brain barreling through yet another schism of time and place but does allow my lungs to gasp in some air.

"This her?"

I don't really hear the asshole's voice but I know it's speaking. And I grasp that it is for some reason speaking about me.

"This Sidonie?"

"Sidonie" is I think, what actually, finally, snaps me out of my stupid-ness. I can still hear Flynn laughing while Imani is trying desperately to hide her hysterics behind her cardboard coffee cup. I manage to realize I should close my mouth and perhaps stand up and mount an attack. Let me be clear, no one calls me Sidonie. No one!

But sadly, life rarely follows the movies. I attempt to move. She, the goddess of my dreams, looks over—and instead of my rising elegantly, and nearly nonchalantly to this occasion, as I have done so many times in my fantasies, I move to unhook my one leg out from under the other and offer up "my name is Sid," all while foisting a withering side glance at Detective whatever-his-name is, when my shoe catches my pants, twisting me into an ungainly tangle, which in turn results in my tossing myself gracelessly backwards in the booth and launching my skinny hot vanilla with whipped cream across the table. Imani lunges to save our vast array of electronic devices and toys while The Mighty Flynn laughs on.

¤ ¤ ¤

Apparently what we had missed, the prelude if you will, is as follows . . .

First, a brief disclaimer, as I was not there. I can only share this part as it was told to me by my former bestie, the now known as Jimmy the-untrustworthy-sod Flynn.

According to Jimmy, he is busy running the tires or tossing footballs or whatever drill thing he is in the middle of when he hears Coach calling him over. Standing with the coach is Mr. Clifton and some guy who looks kind of familiar, but Jimmy can't really place him—and really he isn't trying that hard.

Jimmy jogs his way over and Coach Zaino says, "This is Detective Tsarnowsky. Apparently you met him the other day at the station?"

And as I stated when we first met, my friend Jimmy is the Prince of Judicial Temperament. In this case, that means he pauses and quirks the eyebrow (although this may seem oddly detailed since I was not there, trust me, I am so giving you the short version of Jimmy's blow-by-blow rendition of this momentous event).

So as Jimmy gives Coach, Mr. Clifton and Detective Tsarnowsky his skeptic-not-sure-I-remember eyebrow, Tsarnowsky steps up and addresses Coach without ever taking his eyes off Jimmy. "We didn't actually get a chance to meet, but I did see you," pause, "and your friend. Outside my door."

"Yeah?"

"I heard you and your friend talking about the girl in the picture. I believe your friend, let's see," Tsarnowsky again pauses, gets out his notebook and checks, "Sidonie Rubin," pause, "has an opinion as to what may have happened," his hand now pulls a photo from his notebook, "to our victim that night."

Again, Jimmy relies on his best impassive mode. Probably more cocky than Jimmy will acknowledge, but when you're a big-time quarterback, what would be just plain old snotty if you or I said it somehow still works like a charm.

My Uncle Saul is some super big-time lawyer and when he would come over he would tell me and Jimmy things like, if you walk out of your front door in the morning and you trip over a dead body, call your lawyer before you call the police. My dad would get so annoyed with him and tell us not to listen, but Jimmy always said he was right, that the object of the game is to extract their information without giving yours away. Although I hesitate to state the obvious, I will not be majoring in pre-law.

"Any idea where I might find Sidonie?"

Tsarnowsky inches his way closer to Jimmy, who glances down at the proffered picture and shrugs. "Sorry. Not really sure. I've been here practicing, don't really know where she went."

"Well, do you happen to remember what she was telling you as you peered in the doorway?"

"Not really. Sid was talking. Saying something." Jimmy pauses

19

and lets his eyes catch Mr. Clifton's, serving up a conspiratorial eye roll between those "in the know." "Sid's always talking. I wasn't really listening." And as Jimmy (remember this account comes directly from Himself) is manipulating his way into blowing the detective off, shrugging, smiling his apology as he is reiterating he is in the midst of practice, a woman approaches and, Jimmy relays, his jaw simply stops moving mid-sentence as it drops by like five feet of gape.

Tsarnowsky smiles and introduces his partner, "Detective Macdonald."

Jimmy closes his mouth, hands his helmet to Coach and says, "Gotta go. I just remembered where Sid might be." He takes one more look at the newly arrived Detective Macdonald, laughingly shakes his head, and turns back to Tsarnowsky. "One suggestion. Let her take the lead. Trust me. It will make all the difference in the world."

FOUR

It has taken a bit of maneuvering, but we have trooped and regrouped. We gathered up our gear and left the scene of my shame, sobered up from hilarity so extreme it hurt and we are now resituated two streets down and one avenue across in a booth at the rear of some diner named Platitude. Surveying the scenery, I get the distinct impression this would be a Tsarnowsky choice of venue.

So on the one side of the ring, the three of us sit jammed in together while across from us sit the challengers, Detective Robert Tsarnowsky and Detective Goddess Emma Macdonald. As space in the city is everything, the booths here in Platitude are a bit short and a bit snug and as Tsarnowsky is a bit girth-y, I look across at him and take snide comfort in realizing he is as uncomfortable as we are. At least physically.

We all sit awkwardly posed while the waitress wipes the chipped Formica down with a gray-ish rag that doesn't look like it's any cleaner than the table was to begin with. Then she sets the napkins down onto the still damp table, tosses down some menus, and asks if we are ready or need some time. Tsarnowsky looks expectantly across at us. There are no takers. As if sensing her interruption, she abruptly turns and leaves. Does not even bother with an "I'll check back in a few."

So now that our dynamic waitress has moved on, I feel comfortable sinking back into my holier-than-thou internal snark-fest, trying to make myself feel better at the expense of Tsarno the Barno, when I am again interrupted, this time by my Goddess. "So why don't you tell me Sid... you prefer Sid, right? What was it my

21

partner here thinks he might have overheard?" Then she smiles—at me. Yes me, the smitten kitten. Ah, all I can tell you is it is very hard to mew and speak all at the same time.

But slowly, I began to relate my theory of Tessa Sargentino's death. Well, not exactly a theory about her death, just my theory that she had been out LARPing.

"LARPing?"

"Yeah. Attending a LARP."

"LARP."

"Yeah. Um. A Live Action Role Playing game—LARP." As the words come out, I feel the heat rising in my face again. Can we just scream GEEK now? I can hear the snicker snort of Jimmy and feel his shoulders start to shake again and I try to stem the incoming, raging tide of personal power surge by resorting to a rhyming game I thought I no longer played, "snicker, snicker, snicker, snee, I will kill you like a flea." I thought wrong. Apparently I still play, and apparently it is still not working any better than it did when I was thirteen and in constant exasperation at the obviously moronic world. My knee is tap dancing at an arrhythmic hundred miles an hour, Jimmy's shoulders are convulsing, and I don't know how we didn't just toss Imani sideways, right out from the booth and onto the floor. Let it be said Imani has quite simply not only amazing grace, but apparently also possesses a very low center of gravity.

In an attempt to increase my coordination functions, and settle my escalating pulse, I begin picking at the corner of the plastic-coated menu. Knee Bouncing. Not working. Focus, Sid. Focus!

OMG. If you have never driven on the Highway of Goddess Crush, let me tell you it is a heart-pounding ride. My anxiety-melting Ferrari is whipping by the passing lane for a head-on collision with my adrenaline-rushing Lamborghini.

I mean I ask you, my friend, how would you articulate to the woman you've been crushing on like forever—even though we intellectually do know it's not really her, emotionally and physically your body isn't recognizing that information—how do you tell Detective Goddess Emma Macdonald you're convinced

Tessa Sargentino was coming from a LARP because you looked at a dead body in the newspaper and checked out the ripped bodice of her quality-chosen, well-filled bustier and kind of, sort of, recognized, not her, but it. I am so freakin' cruising straight down the rabbit hole.

This is so not how I imagined . . . you know, I think we can just stop there. Let that thought be complete just as is. Honestly, this is so not how I imagined anything. I'm not sure in my wildest thinking I could have even come close to imagining whatever this is. OMG! Kill me now!

¤ ¤ ¤

But the sad fact is, not only can't you die from mortification, most people you know can't even kill you over it. They are too busy laughing way too hard at you.

So here we are, sitting in a booth, everybody twitching, waiting for me to expound, but as I said, it honestly, truly wasn't really much of a theory, just that I figured she, Tessa Sargentino, was out LARPing and that was kind of it.

And with that, I shrugged and jammed my hands in between my knees so I might ward off all sorts of chills as I sat waiting for the expected. For the life slap I know is coming. For Tsarno the Barno, to pull his over-fed, fat self up and go, taking my walking vision away with him. And so I sit and I wait, but rather shockingly the slap never comes.

Instead, they let the silence build until I find myself doing exactly what I told myself I would not do, explaining defensively. "Understand LARPing is not some simple masquerade or costume ball or some kind of weird Halloween party. It is a live action role-playing game, which means you not only inhabit the character you are playing, but everyone in the LARP has their own roles to play and we are all parts of a greater whole." As I pause for a second, letting that thought finish thrusting off my tongue and into their ears, I realize I now know how to get myself through this moment.

I am having a brainstorm or maybe just a brain fart. Hard to say.

I will utilize my not quite finely honed LARPing skills to craft a character. I will call her "Sid the Kid" because she will be like Clint Eastwood back in the day: part outlaw, all chiseled charm. And when Sid the Kid is finished, she will ride off into the sunset with an indelible flourish, leaving them (although let's be honest, don't really care about him whatsoever, as it is only about leaving her) enlightened and starstruck. And as Sid the Kid rises up, she elucidates, "It's mythologic not just thematic."

Très cray cray I know.

So now I work my western outlaw nonchalance—shifting in my seat, draping my arm over the back of the booth—and I raise my eyes, hoping they are squinting as perfectly as Clint's, and buoyed by my newfound sangfroid, which is one of my favorite French words (merci Mama!) whose generic translation would be calmness, as in buoyed by my newfound calmness, but whose literal translation is cold blood (how perfect is that!) I continue, "LARPing is a type of social storytelling. It is not only bringing a story to life; it is using group inspiration and wit to write chapters and volumes and spinoffs and sequels without ownership or corporate interference. It is an incredibly pure art form as it is only as good as the people who show up to invest themselves and their character."

Whew.

I pause for a breath and realize, oddly enough being Sid the Kid does seem to resonate while delivering a share of good news and bad news. Good news is I am now in control, commanding their attention. Bad news, judging by the stares, I think I am being perceived as less Cool Clint than a three-headed troglodyte. And while I definitely believe there are troglodytes among us, I resent thinking they could be thinking I might be one. However, Tsarno, who truly might be one, has at least finally stopped snorting. *Oh yeah, that's the way to make my day!* I blow my imaginary pistol, twirl, and holster.

Cheap thrill. What can I say?

24

Oh no. Excuse me but I must break off my own internal, pat-on-my-back, mini-rant as Goddess Emma is asking another question.

"And who organizes this LARP?"

"Uh, the Game Master." Again. Blank stares. "Okay, I mean it isn't a specific person I can tell you, like John Smith organized it. Anyone can be a game master; that's just the title given to the person whose LARP it is. And there are all kinds of LARPs. Some LARPs might play out over three or four days, some are just hours, and some evolve over weeks or months. So if you're a game master, you have to determine what kind of LARP you are organizing. You have to set the mythos of it all . . . uhm . . . the narrative theme. And then you have to set characters and parameters and and and."

"Okay, so how would we find the Game Master?"

"It's pretty much not that hard. They're the ones running the game. I mean they have NPCs, non-player characters to help them, but they're more like employees. So kind of like any company, they can direct you to the GM." You know, it never had occurred to me before, but it's really kind of funny that larps are all about non-ownership, but when you shorthand—Game Master and General Manager and, duh, General Motors, all shorthand into GM. (Okay, might be a digression, but really so small as to qualify as a mini-digression at best. It just struck me as funny for a moment. Perhaps ironic might be a better term. And it was just a moment. Sheesh. Continuing on.)

"Okay. In a basic sense, I'm a GM and I'm going to host a LARP. I decide I'm doing a wedding LARP. Two warring families will be joined through this union. The problem is the ring has been stolen, and without the ring there can be no wedding. The Quest will be to save the day by finding the ring. So who is at the wedding that could have stolen it? Could it be the jilted ex? The drug-addicted bartender? Could it be the father of the bride or maybe the mother of the groom? Maybe they don't want this war that has plagued the families to end. And if I make it an Edwardian LARP, maybe it is Romeo and Juliet, but if I make it

Americana, maybe it's Hatfields and McCoys. If I make it Medieval Fantasy, maybe no one wants a mixed marriage between an Elf and a Dwarf, or if it's a Space Opera, maybe, just maybe it's the wedding of Captain Kirk to an alien race in an arranged marriage, which could save the universe as we know it," I pause here for dramatic effect, "except the ring is missing, people!"

I would love to say this was a great example. Truth is, not so much. But it does seem to make the basics if not quite understandable, at least somewhat accessible. There seems to be a bit of nodding and shuffling and then what will be the one last question from the Goddess: did I know who was hosting a LARP last week? Most likely somewhere near Bryant Park?

"No."

And just like that, we were done. Tsarno called the waitress back, asked for a coffee and the bill and then pulled out some cash without waiting for either. With a thank you at the door and a quick shoulder squeeze from my Goddess, they were gone.

I do know I just stood there for a minute. I am guessing I was touching my shoulder with great reverence, because I honestly forgot to breathe, so I'm not 100 percent positive of everyone's comings and goings, but then I remember Imani shrieking she is going to be killed if she doesn't get home, "like now!" so we all grabbed our jackets and electronics and stuff and we raced with her to the subway.

After she left, I thought me and The Flynn would get to download together, but no, my descent into weirdness was not yet over. As we turn to walk home, Jimmy says, "Hey Sid?"

"Yeah?"

"I want to ask Imani if she'll go out with me."

"Out with you?" I stop walking for a minute, put my arm out to stop him, move my body in front of him so I can look at him straight on. I need to make sure I just heard this right. That some taxicab didn't honk right over what he was saying and set my hearing abilities askew. "As in out like out on a date? Like one on one?"

"Yeah."

Wow. Hand to forehead I spin a 360. Wowzerhole. This one I did not see coming. I mean why should I? I just want to stand here in the middle of the street and scream. This is so not fair. There's a whole school of people out there. If I was at home right now and Jimmy was texting me this, I would just wait for the winking smiling emoticon I would be sure was coming. Then I could grumpily text back red face, pause for a minute to smirk, and then go back to whatever I was doing thinking, *funny, Flynn, funny. You're just a laugh a minute.* Only that isn't what's happening. There is no winking smiley here.

So I look up at The Flynn, who is now standing in front of me with his hands smushed down in his pockets and I try and picture Imani standing with him, her arm linked through his, wearing her hip pleather jacket and F'Ugg Boots, both of them laughing at something impossibly funny that only they could get.

Big sigh. Some asshole leans on his horn as though that will actually get him somewhere faster. The smell of the pretzels and sewer combination wafts past me. There's a strange comfort in it. I just don't understand; why does my best friend need to ask out my other best friend? It's not like best friends just grow on trees. What happens if they go out and decide they hate each other? What if they go out and they decide they like each other so much there's no room for anyone else? Not even me.

And then again, it's not like I'm going to date him. And it's not like I'm going to date her. And it's not like they haven't dated lots of other people. But they didn't count. They were just OPs, other people. But Jimmy and Imani? They're my best friends. And what if they somehow leave me behind? Will I be left all alone?

But as I look at Jimmy, looking at me, all nervous and expectant, I can't say any of this. All I can do is shrug and say, "Sure." But as much as I wish I could tell you I so do not give a fluck, truth is, my heart breaks just a smidge.

FIVE

And because Imani said yes, I am now spending Saturday night sitting alone at a back bar table in a local and, well, what you might call rather sketchy watering hole, feeling a little bit pissy. And maybe just a wee bit sorry for myself as I pretend I am not drowning my sorrows, all while sipping my orange juice on ice and playing obsessively with the wet corner of my napkin. And since orange juice will not dull one's senses, I am unfortunately not so far gone, and therefore quite capable of espying one Vikram Patel holding the door open for the grand entrance of one larger than life of the party, Arianna Wilson, better known to us all as Ari.

I thought about ducking, but it was too late. I could hear the shriek.

"Sid!" Ari has managed to spot me and is now making a bee-line straight for me. I watch with amazement as the crowd quite simply makes room for Ari. I mean if you've ever seen any movie whereby Moses parts the Red Sea—trust me, he had to work harder than she is.

"Finally." Breathlessly Ari leans in over the table, allowing her rather remarkable double Ds to practically soak up the condensation near my glass. "I told Vikram we needed to find you. That if Jimmy and Imani are suddenly an item, you will need your pals to get you through this adjustment. And don't bother with the 'I'm fine' bullshit."

I somehow manage not to move and not to inhale, torn between self-consciousness as to where my exhaled inhale would land and fear of using the comfort offered to lean in, burrow deep, and just lose control. Fortunately, before Ari notices my new mannequin act, she steps back so I can both breathe and follow her emphatic hand gestures as she ticks off my slittany aka sin litany.

"You are not responding to my texts," her left thumb hooks the air, "you are looking like a mess," index finger, and oh, a sweep into the pointer, which reverses and charges at me, "and not a hot one," the jabbing pointer continues, "and" look out, the Ds are on the move again, inhale and freeze, "your hulk and sulk is truly killing the atmo here. I think the bar would happily pay *me* the five-buck cover just to get you out. Although, I have to say, you do worry me, Sid. Who the fuck goes out on a *literary* pub crawl in order to sulk? I mean I figured it out in like ten minutes because once I thought about it, I realized only Sid Rubin would think Hemingway would be a perfect companion to go drown her sorrows with."

I could see how to the uninitiated this might sound callous, but not if you know Ari. Whenever I get close enough to be in her orbit, I have to always remember to close my mouth. I honestly like Ari, always have. But 1) she always just kind of leaves me half stunned and 2) I just cannot understand what she sees in Vikram? Why she needs him?

I mean Ari just exudes magnetism and, well, sex. She is one of those sheer forces of personality, big girls. A jolt-laden, quantum physics, double shot of energy and pizazz and, well, sex. When Ari tosses back her multicolored hair (think of blue and pink intermingled in an array of blonds) and laughs, you are happy to be there even if you don't get the joke. She makes you believe the party is wherever she is. She can say anything and just get away with it because she is Arianna Wilson—one big girl with one big personality (and two, let me just say, again, two really big breasts) and one big belief in herself and it all works.

Vikram, on the other hand, I find to be a loser, and I mean loser with a capital L. He's really skinny, and he has these sort of sunken, raccoon-y like eyes and well, he kind of twitches. You

30

know, he's the guy whose hand you don't want to shake 'cause you just know it's going to be clammy, never mind the idea that those hands could be touching anything else. Blech. Yuck. Ugh. Gives me the creeps. And I guess I could, in a kind, weak-hearted moment, think maybe there's more to Vikram than I am seeing, but I just can't see how Ari actually went out—in public—with him before making him, thankfully, lose the emo flap. That is the true mystery to me. Of and by itself, that emo flap was the reason why any seeing person, never mind vibrant Ari, would have turned him down.

So, between you and me, I will admit that one day when we were randomly alone in the hallway, I was overcome by a total need to know and thus I did ask Ari, "Vikram, really?" and she explained their attraction to me as follows, "You know, Sid, he has it all: big brains and big, ahem, other attributes."

OMG. Way TMI for me, but I had asked. And then, then she wasn't done 'splaining. Ari leaned in really close until I could feel her breath on my ear and her hair tickle my cheek, and trust me, none of that was by accident. My pulse skyrocketed, my body left my mind way behind, and I knew she not only knew it, she was making sure I was closing in on exploding.

"And me, Sid?" Ari dropped her voice really low, licked her lips (I'm pretty sure they actually licked my ear, but that might have been wishful thinking). "I want it all—every single inch of it. So it works," and before I could get under control, her tongue was in my mouth and then out barreled that laugh, "for me." Yep. Mouth agape. Mine.

I did mention she is possessed of a rather large, playful per-sonality.

And while you might be inclined to dismiss all this as simply an entertaining digression, it truly is not. It is a sharing of peeps and personalities who might fall under your need to know as we continue our journey.

You're welcome.

Argh! Before I remember I should answer Ari and stop speaking with you, my friends, Vikram reappears not only with

31

beers in hand, he has somehow managed to snag an extra stool and thus my fate is sealed. Sealed because although I am obviously alone, I cannot very well tell them they can't sit down. Not when they have brought their own stools. Never mind that I probably would have told them to sit anyway, but at least I would have been able to ignore them if they did sit down—if I were here with my buds. But I'm not with my buds because they are with each other. And yes, I am thinking of ordering some cheese with that whine.

¤ ¤ ¤

Okay, Sid. Get it together. Enough with this personal pity party. Velma would not approve. Remove your glasses. Squint your eyes. Scrunch your nose. Okay. Inhale. Exhale. Glasses back onto their bridge. It is time to regain some semblance of control.

"So," I fiercely push the shredded pile formerly called a napkin away and move from my head out into the newly assembled, thrusting forward, slipping into my cloak of deflection, determined to assert my leadership and not quietly shirk my way into mute acceptance of a new, unasked for status, that of a sitting duck to my own wake. "So, just for the record, you're wrong, Ari. You know, I mean, when you assumed Hemingway is why I'd be here. It's not Hemingway. It's Virginia Woolf. As in," pause for dramatic effect, "'thinking is my fighting.'"

Deep. Kind of genius, don't you think?

Or not.

Because following a rather deliberate, pregnant pause of non-response—during which Ari studiously ignores my insight and glances sadly over to Vikram, shakes her head and then, turns back—she reaches for my hand. I gaze about in an effort to determinedly not snatch my hand back, all while manufacturing an appearance of equal parts studiously heady and laid-back cool. In spite of my faked nonchalance I am obviously not fooling these two. And just when one of us would be obligated to make some type of next move, smack, right in line with my sudden-onset affliction, you know, the one with the very scientific name, the Peculiar-Twists-of-Fate, this hand dance of shared grief is abruptly overtaken by an interloper, a shadow crossing right over our table, looking to cut in. The eerie presence grows larger as shadow merges with flesh and an oddly familiar and previously described girth consumes our table. My tilt-a-whirl button spins left, right, and upside down.

Yes, it is (drumroll please) the reappearance of the amazing Tsarno the Barno and, well, let's just say "ask" would be way more polite than it is, but okay, after gazing dismissively at my current company he "asks" me to join him outside. I mean, "ask" would imply I had a choice. Somehow I do not think this request is exactly optional.

We slog our way to the door and step toward the curb, passing through the smoke brigade the exiled puffers have raised. Tsarno the Barno turns toward me. "You know that's an establishment which serves liquor?"

I want to preface this next detail with "I am incredibly proud of myself." I actually thought before I spoke. Now granted, all my thoughts might be categorized as "smart assed." For example, I thought I could say, "gee, really?" I also thought I could say, "Wow, you must be really observant." Or maybe, "Now I know why they call you Detective." I thought so many things at once it was like I was flying on my own snide high. They were all actually screaming "pick me, pick me" and yet, somehow, I found control I did not know I had. Somehow I beat them all back into the recesses of my brain, choking them away from my mouth, and swallowing them up, the only trace evidence they ever existed being the quirk of my brow.

He stands there and motions. I ignore the wet chill in the air, the water still dripping from the higher floors right down onto us, determined to remain blasé as I give him the ID. And again, I am proud of myself for not pointing out I could make fifty more before the night is through. I am just sharing that even I know certain boasts will not get me what I seek—whatever that may be. At this point, I don't know.

"So," Tsarno looks over the ID, "pretty decent job here." I watch as he flips it about between his fingers, seemingly thinking. Decision reached, the flipping stops, and he hands it back to me.

Again, I say nothing, although I must admit I am rather surprised. I retrieve my ID and return it to my flip, back-pocket wallet with as much baby dyke savoir faire as I can muster. If he is expecting anything else, he will not get it. You see, I possess an important piece of wisdom. I know rule number one from my days back at the Kindergarten Corral: Do not, under any circumstances, take candy from a stranger. I am not biting.

And as we stand here, feinting and parrying with looks and half starts, we become two prizefighters warily deciding where our left hooks might reach and where they might leave us exposed. Oh, fuck me. Now all I can hear is the theme song to *Rocky* turning on in that radio in my brain. Shit.

As if sensing he has a momentary advantage, Tsarno throws down, playing his opening gambit. "I did a bit of checking you out." Pause. Pause. "Interesting incident you had there in the sixth grade."

And let me tell you, the sucker punch lands. I never saw it coming. My breath sucks in, my eyes double in size, and my body nearly doubles over. I stagger a step back and before I can get enough oxygen to my brain to think anything, I hear, through my mental haze, someone screaming "Sid, Sid," and tearing down the street, gaining substance and power with each light he passes under, charging, racing, my knight in shining armor, followed by a team of screaming squires. "Sid, don't say anything. Tell him nothing."

And as he arrives, Jimmy takes one look at me and sees what I do not, the fear and the tears starting to well. Not tears of sadness, tears of emotion. The Flynn turns and wheels at Tsarno, "What did you do to her?!"

Tsarno stands there, looking as aghast as I am feeling. I reach for Jimmy's arm, pulling his ear next to my lips. "He knows, Jimmy. He knows all about sixth grade."

SIX

We traipse our way back to the bowel of what is seemingly becoming "our booth" in the lovely environs of Platitude. And if I thought five of us crammed in had been a tight squeeze, six is not a party (and that would be before factoring in Tsarno's width and Ari's curves). If Vikram wasn't so obnoxiously skinny and able to be stuffed between Ari and Tsarno and if I had been able to sit up straight and stop cowering in Jimmy's armpit (while Imani seemed to need to snuggle on his other side—just sayin') we probably wouldn't have made it.

And when the plastic-coated menus hit the table, and a voice says, "what will it be?" I realize this is really happening. Bizarrely, I recognize this voice and with great reluctance, but compelled to do so, I manage to shift my nose right, freeing up an eyeball just enough to peer and confirm. I so badly want to grab my cell phone and change my calendar entry for today to the *Twilight Zone* ring tone. Yes, my friends, you guessed it. It is, ironically, the same waitress from what is unbelievably only this afternoon. I would say wow, what déjà vu, but that would be wrong. Déjà vu would be the sense of having a glimpse of having been here, when I actually have a reality of having been here. And actually, technically not the same waitress as this afternoon, she actually is the same waitress from yesterday, as it's now twelve thirty in the morning. So same day, or next day, depending on how you want to factor the midnight hour.

And no, I am not dithering here. I am honestly trying to force my brain to reconcile it was only ten hours ago I was first here.

But then, while I am shifting, seeking confirmation for my befuddled brain, our eyes meet and I suddenly realize just how bad a shape I must be in, because she, the wan, overworked waitress, teems with sympathy. I swear I even think I can hear her clucking, but I am guessing that's probably in my head.

All right, so that's enough PTOing (Personal Time Out-ing for anyone who might not read initials) Sometimes in order to go forward, one must go back. So without further ado . . .

. . . The Incident of the Sixth Grade. Wow. Where to begin?

As I previously mentioned, Jimmy always seems to suffer from judicial temperament, while I am afflicted with it-seemed-like-such-a-good-idea-at-the-time disease.

Anyway, because we go to a smallish private school, we don't have the usual issues about graduating from a grade school and starting all over again in junior high and then again for high school. If you get in and survive the third-grade cut, you are in unless you do something incredibly stupid. And in New York City, where most kids have to apply for a high school, this has definite perks. But we also don't get any graduation fanfare. No assembly. No pomp. No circumstance. And let's be honest, since we are a bunch of preteens, this no assembly, no little, tacky graduation ceremony really means No Gifts. And there was this group of us sitting on the steps leading up to the front hallway, Jimmy and myself included, who got into a conversation about how it isn't fair that the school doesn't do anything to mark this transition. Not even some kind of announcement. Nothing. And then the bell rang, and then we went back to class.

And that was that.

Well, at least until about two in the morning when I was still up, wide awake and hitting the overtired wall where all jokes are hilarious and all ideas are genius. Now if you were an adult and you weren't an insomniac kid simply wired to do stupid, you would go to sleep and in the morning realize that all your hilarious, genius thinking was kind of dumb and that would be that. But if you happen to be in an insomniac's high state and, as noted earlier, lack any meaningful brain development, now, *now* you are wide open to doubling down on your lack of good consequence reasoning with brilliance you are defining by exhaustive giddiness. And well let's just say, the term genius is, ahem, bitterly laced with double-edged irony.

And so it came to be, at two in the morning on this fateful day, I sat up and wrote what was honestly a very simple script, congratulating everyone in the sixth grade on their accomplishment and boosting their averages by cleverly adding an "A" for the effort it took to get here. I then texted my genius to The Flynn, but he didn't answer, so I guessed he was sleeping. I read my note again, quite literally added a bell and a whistle (it was a personally amusing touch) determined it was now perfect, and of course brilliant, and thus, with a flourishing stroke or two of my keyboard, injected the note and its accompanying Bonus "A" coding right onto the school's computer system.

I climbed into bed, grinning, fully satiated. It was a great night.

As you might have already guessed, it was not to be a great morning.

A couple of years ago Jimmy and I had worked out an "emergency signal" between us, which we had never used. You see, we both had cell phones, but they came with a list of rules. One of those rules was I could not keep my cell phone in the bedroom. It had to go to a family docking station after I got home from school and if friends wanted to talk to me, they could call the house line. It sucked.

If however, there is one upside to all the homework a private school demands—something I personally think is done solely to ensure parents feel they are getting their money's worth—it means having a computer in my bedroom became a kind of necessity. And while I was not deemed old enough to be on certain websites, I was allowed to be on what was called the "school loop." A lovely place where both students and their parents could log on to read the school paper (that would be the student part) or check what homework had been assigned (that would be your parents' portion). It's amazing how well honor systems work when you take the ability to lie right off the table.

Although I still don't think if you can get your math home-work done during history, you should be penalized.

Anyway, I was allowed to be on a browser, which was kind of all Jimmy and I needed to create our very own secure online world. And within that world, we built an emergency beacon of our own, which we had never used, until today.

I awoke to Jimmy's voice in my bedroom saying, "Emergency. Emergency." My first instinct was to pull the blanket over my head and tell him to shut up. So I did. Then I realized he wouldn't be in my bedroom saying "Emergency." So then I was up and online, my hair sticking out every which way, my glasses kind of on top of my head, my heart pounding so fast, so loud. My toe throbbed, not from my head, but from the corner of the desk I rammed it into trying to pull up the hidden folder.

I opened the folder, managing to type our secret passphrase NuCLEArOpT!oN77 in spite of my finger's sudden inability to recognize brain signals. I so wished I could get my toe up to my mouth so I could suck on it and stop the hurt. Maybe if I pushed down on it with my other foot. The pounding in my head was making me nauseous.

The scroll came up just as we had designed. Line after line of code. Two hundred lines before the code would become false. And here it was:

xxnygxcdksbcxxvyllixx

You see, we built what were called While Loops. And after we determined when they would go false, they would then provide the clue to the key which would unlock this code, which in turn would tell us which one of twelve possible meeting places we were to head to ASAP.

Okay. So there's the code. It reads, "Hail Caesar N10."

Which is a designed standard Caesarian Shift Cipher Encoder. Basically one of those wheel ciphers where there is an inner wheel with the alphabet around the outside and you place it on an outer wheel with the alphabet going around it.

But I don't have a wheel and obviously we have an emergency. So I grab paper and start making a list of the alphabet the long

38

way. Then I grab another piece of paper and do it again. I take the letter N on the first piece and then count ten letters down so that finally I have the key. N = X. Double xx's are to be ignored.

xxnygxcdksbcxxvyllixx
xxdownstairsxxlobbyxx

Downstairs. Lobby. Holy Moly. Here. The Flynn is here. Downstairs. This is bad. Bad. Pull on pants. Sneakers. No. No Sneakers. School day. Loafers. Teeth brushing can wait. Sweater. On. Go. Now.

And I grab my bag and run. I spin headfirst into a wall that wasn't there just yesterday. It is a wall formed by an unsmiling Mom and Dad, and if I thought I was feeling nauseous and had an idea this is not going to be a good morning, now I know I am going to throw up. My dad calmly reaches over and takes my backpack and says, "Why don't you go see if Jimmy wants to ride to school with us."

Ride. As in "we will take the car" and not call a cab. We don't do that unless we are visiting Dad's parents or some other road trip. No. We are city people. We take subways and buses and the occasional taxi. This is bad. Really bad.

So there we are, me and Jimmy (Jean having been ordered to get moving and take the subway) huddling in the backseat of the car, at least as much as two people buckled into their seat belts can huddle, trying to catch each other up—sort of. Think hushed, urgent whispers, all while being eyed by Dad in the rear view mirror while Mom sits in the front seat, her arms wrapped around herself.

"Sid," Jimmy's whisper is more like a hiss, "you didn't, did you?"

"What."

"Sid."

Okay, my life is spiraling on a downward trajectory. I went to bed expecting The Flynn to fist bump me in some manner, but even he is looking serious and sick and suddenly speaking so he sounds a lot like my dad.

"I thought it would be funny."

"Oh no, Sid." Jimmy went from noticeably twitchy to looking like he was going to cry. "Hacking isn't funny."

"Hacking?"

"That's what it's called. Hacking. Like breaking and entering. Only it's hacking."

"But I wasn't hacking," my voice cracks as my brain finally catches up with why I am in so much trouble. And even as I say it, I know my excuse is going to be lame, but yet I croak on, "I was just posting."

And with that admission, the worst day of my life got even worse. And it wasn't because I had just been labeled a hacker and apparently I could go to jail. No, that was all just technical stuff. But in the backseat of my Dad's Benz, Jimmy Flynn looked at me as if I was an idiot, as if he could not believe I, Sid Rubin, could possibly be this stupid. And that hurt more than even how scared I was.

By now we had pulled up at the school and standing, waiting in the parking lot, were Flynn's parents. Together we embarked upon what I was sure was my own private Bataan Death March down what I was also sure was the world's longest hallway. I still don't understand how a body moves forward when the only two words left that sound right are *run now*.

But I didn't run. And I did force my feet to keep up.

And then nothing could have prepared me for what happened next. Kapow. Wham. Bam. The ground shook and not only don't I think I have ever felt so loved in my life, I know I have never been so in awe.

So what caused this heaven and earthshaking moment?

Picture this. Me, having arrived at the office at the end of the hall, now half-standing, all-trembling, in front of Principal Saffitz who was nastily pontificating my sins—how I had hacked into the system, how it was a criminal offense, how the police had to be called, how I obviously was not cut out for this school—during which I tried to focus on his ear hair in an effort not to cry, when, from behind me I heard my dad quietly say, in that same tone of voice he uses when he's not happy with what

40

I am about to do, "No." To which my mom replied, a little less quietly, "Chut." And then as one might say, it was game on.

There is a French expression, "bête belle" and its translation is "monster pretty" and wow, she so was. I mean, in that moment, I saw my mother in a whole new light. This time there was nothing, uhm, what's the word I want? I don't know. Coquettish, I guess. Remember when I mentioned to you all about how when Mom gets "all French," she wins. Well, *this* French was not to be confused with *that* French. This French was neither flirtatious nor playful. And it was most definitely not seductive. This French was a whole new French, fiery and majestic and *très*, *très* imperious. My mom, the bête belle, had no hint of a Collette or a Cosette. No. My mom became the worthy heir to the Queen of "Let Them Eat Cake and Off With Their Heads," the ultimate bête belle personified, Marie Antoinette.

She "pardoned" her interruption, but just was curious, "what would be the point of the school if they … hmmmm … evicted, oui, their best and their brightest? Isn't that the school's entire raison d'être? Wouldn't that be precisely why the parents have chosen to associate their children here?"

Open the floodgates, let the accented torrent flow! Kapow!

By the time Mom came up for air, even I was starting to feel just the tiniest bit sorry for Principal Saffitz. He was sadly way out of his league. And then, just in case he had somehow managed to miss the point, up steps Mrs. Flynn who adds, "if you cannot find a way to make this an opportunity for a *teaching* moment, then we, too, would have our child in the wrong school. It would just seem to me, that a prank which hurt no one, but was obviously quite simply juvenile and ill-conceived, would provide a perfect moment in time, and opportunity, to *educate* our children rather than make a criminal out of the child and erase her from your sight, just so you might wipe out the offending situation," and here she paused, "until, of course, it next arises."

With that, Jimmy and I were sent outside while the grown-ups cut the deal. I had to be suspended for three days, during which time I was to prepare a three-page essay on the ethics of hacking and deliver it upon my return to a full—from Kindergarten to Twelfth Grade—school assembly. I was then on probation for the next year. After that, this incident would be sealed and not part of my permanent record.

That assembly was, and still is, the hardest day of my life.

"Still is?" you ask. Yes. Still is. Because, as sadly noted from an earlier incident, somehow stupid never grows old, and now, as every school year begins, there is an assembly to discuss ethics and some idiot always yells out, "it's time for this year's edition of 'Ethics with Sid.'" Jimmy actually suggested this year I should show up for school wearing ashes and a sackcloth. Which might have been hysterical, if he and I had been speaking about OPs, other people. But we weren't. So to put it succinctly, this falls under the category of "still too soon to be funny."

And, because who doesn't like a little salt poured into their wounds, it of course wasn't even sophisticated enough to include in my APP Portfolio so I could salvage something from my pain, if not my pride.

But even with nothing salvaged, I did survive that day and all its annual cousins and I have successfully managed to otherwise never spend time thinking about it. Until tonight. When Tsarno the Barno sucker-punched me.

And now, having finished my confession I realize it is time to rejoin the present, so naturally, just as I look up, a chair is dropped at the head of the table, directly to my right, long legs swing over it and a voice says, "So, is she in?" and I look up into the eyes of Detective Goddess Emma Macdonald and I know, whatever it is, I am so in.

SEVEN

Which got more fully explained the following morning at nine o'clock sharp when Detectives Tsarnowsky and Macdonald arrived to see my parents and pay them an, I don't know, social call, kind of. But not really. It was more of a business call, which actually was, in a nutshell, all about borrowing me to do a bit of computer excavating for them, on LARPS.

I am guessing my parents knew something funny was up, if for no reason other than the fact that not only was I wide awake at eight A.M. on a Sunday MORNING—redundancy intentional. I was up, showered, fully dressed with effort and purpose, wearing my birthday Levi's which I got to have custom tailored for myself at the Levi's store, and practicing relaxing downstairs with a large cup of coffee, poured from the pot I had personally measured and brewed.

Again. All this. Voluntarily. At eight o'clock on a Sunday morning.

And so, here comes Mom strolling out of her bedroom, wearing her Sunday loungewear (lightweight drawstring bottoms, tank top, no bra, no makeup) and with a quirk of her eyebrow, saunters to the coffee pot. As she begins pouring her coffee, we are both very fake-still and quiet. I practice playing "Feigning My Nonchalance" and pick up a section of our Sunday *NY Times* to not actually peruse.

I throw down by taking a sip of coffee, adjusting my newspaper to better use my skilled sideways glancing. I watch as Mom takes a good minute to, oh so casually, prep her coffee, first adding, then

43

stirring her cream, deliberately placing the spoon in the sink, blowing across the top, taking a small, cautious sip, and then casually turning to me. Slowly she makes her way over, ostensibly to kiss me good morning on the top of my head, but actually, before I can twist, she uses her hand like a vise to catch hold of my chin, tilt my head up until my eyes meet hers, and peer.

Uh Oh.

She then says, "The food section, Sidonie? I must say, an excellent choice. But really, so very unlike you."

Trump. So busted.

So when I kind of half-shrug, half-grimace, 'cause really, what else am I going to do, she takes her still attached to my chin hand and shakes it gently, "Ah, Sidonie, I presume I will find out soon, oui?"

And before I can even reply, as if on cue, the buzzer provides her answer.

I move to jump up, but she stays me with that one raised eyebrow, accompanied by a wag of her finger and a, "tut, tut."

"Oui?"

"Um, hello. Mrs. Rubin?" As Tsarno's disembodied voice begins booming into our quiet apartment, I realize how nervous I had been, not from waiting on Tsarno and not because of the approaching task at hand, but from thinking I had somehow made all this up. That last night had actually been just some kind of whacked-out dream. Which not only would be kind of psycho-ward scary, but which kind of would have been very humiliating. I mean, what would I say? "Hey thanks for all the attention, but turns out I have no story to tell. Or forget LARPing with Sid; we're flying psychotropic instead." Talk about wowzerhole.

So it is actually with what you might call a big ungainly gasp of relief that I listen to the voice boom through the static: "Uh, yes, ma'am, my name is Detective Robert Tsarnowsky and I was hoping you had a minute to talk to us, um, that would be myself and my partner, Detective Emma Macdonald, about your daughter, Sidonie."

Mom doesn't even reply; she simply hits the buzzer. Then she looks at me. "I'll put something else on and get your father." As she opens the bedroom door, she turns back. "A little warning might have been nice, Sidonie."

¤   ¤   ¤

My dad leans forward in the armchair he has chosen, his hands clasped together, dangling between his legs, "Just so we understand this correctly, Sid had a . . ." he pauses for a minute, his middle fingers rocking back and forth as if he is getting ready to play here's the church and here's the steeple. What he is really doing is trying to absorb the story by talking. We are a family possessed of many great verbal processors. His fingers move back and forth, finally stilling as he finds the word he wants, "a *theory* about a murdered woman, which she discussed while on her school-approved police station visit? A theory you think might have merit, so you want her to come down to the station today and help you sort data in order to prove her theory and help you catch the murderer?"

Before either detective could reply, I jump in, hurriedly clarifying, "Not just me, Dad. Me and Jimmy."

"Oh really." Dad is so not impressed with my interruption. He returns his attention to the detectives. "Has Mrs. Flynn agreed to this?"

"Not yet, Mr. Rubin," Detective Goddess Emma Macdonald gently smiles over to me, which causes me to both blush and beam, although thankfully everyone else is way too intent on talking *about* me, rather than *to* me, to notice. "As this was Sid's theory, our first stop was here. We're hoping you'll agree to let her help us out and then we plan to head over to Jimmy's house and hopefully enlist him as well."

"Hmmmm. I see."

Dad exchanges glances with mom, looks at the detectives, looks at me seemingly searching for something I can only hope he is getting, and then he stands. "Excuse us for a moment please."

45

And with that, he and Mom head off for a private pow-wow, leaving me with the detectives. If this were a bad movie, the only sound track playing would be a deafening ticking clock.

Tick. Tick. Tick.

I sit with my legs crossed at the ankles in an effort to keep my knee from insanely bobbing up and down, so instead my right ankle takes over this reasonably uncontrolled rhythm. I take some comfort in observing how uncomfortable Tsarno looks. Sadly for the big guy, he got the ever so slightly saggy cushion and sat down about an inch after it lost perch-ability—he's not rocking a good look. Goddess Emma, of course, looks fine. Mighty fine, really. Unfortunately, she signals Tsarno she is stepping outside to return a call, leaving me and Tsarno Barno alone.

Which means, I realize, I am now suddenly somehow the unofficial hostess here, but let's be honest, this is so not in my skill set. I mean we can acknowledge I can talk a blue streak with the best of them. The logical extension of these traits might be a talent for small talk. But it's not. And, yes, I can digress with the best, but stalling, not so much. I stumble, I stammer, I suck. But in an attempt to rise to this challenge, I hunt for a topic, trying them on sort of like "Does this shirt go with these pants?"

Wrack the brain. Maybe I could snap my fingers and try a nonchalant, "Hey, did you know the act of snapping one's fingers has a name? It's called a fillip. Just in case you were ever wondering and needed to know." Oh boy, lame. And do not, I say to myself, do not start playing your nails as though they are some kind of musical washboard instrument.

Plucking another thought from the loop of random running about, "You know, I'm thinking of building an urban bird house to put on the outside of my window. Well, build might not be technically correct. I am actually 3D printing it from an open source design." Ooh yeah, there's some real bonding material there, Sid. Give yourself a nice snort.

Pffft. I glance over at the hulk perched on the edge of our couch, just as he moves his hands forward. Lace the fingers. Bend them back. And. Crack. It's a strike! All eight at once. Although

I guess that's technically a spare. Wow. It is resoundingly loud in the absolute stillness we have created. Loud enough I think, to bring my parents running. But apparently not.

Tick. Tick. The air is thick with tick. I pun, I do. Wow. I really have nothing. Crack. Wrack. Wrack the brain. Wait I got something. Maybe. Perhaps. "Did you know there was a recent scientific study whose purpose was to determine how the noise is made from the act of cracking one's knuckles, an art I see you excel in?"

Okay, on third thought, another nonstarter.

"Words are the tools of imagery in motion." That's one of my favorite quotes. It's by Sam Shepard. You know how some things you hear and they just stick? It's like my other favorite quote, "oozing charm from every pore, he oiled his way across the floor." That's George Bernard Shaw and it's from his play, *Pygmalion*. We read it in seventh grade. I think I love it mostly because there's this creepy, smiley guy in Apartment 1C and when we read the play and got to that line, it made me think of the slimy perv. Mom asks me not to call him that, but she also told us to stay away from him. And so now, every time I pass the guy, all I can hear is "oozing charm from every pore . . ."

Tick. Tick. Tock. Tock. OMG. I hear a lock! They finally open the door!

I don't know who is more relieved, me or Barno? We both jump at the sound.

The parents come into the room and Dad waits for Detective Tsarnowsky to haul himself out of the couch while once again giving his best scrutinizing once-over. "Just some computer help?"

"Yes."

Mom. Hands crossed over her chest. "We expect her back in time for dinner."

"Shouldn't be a problem. Thank you. We really appreciate your letting Sidonie help us out. A pleasure to have met you both."

And with a handshake of agreement, Tsarno turns to me and nods he will be outside waiting, quickly taking his leave along with his yes for an answer.

And we don't lose any time rounding up The Flynn, because, of course, my parents hadn't agreed to anything until they had called Mr. and Mrs. Flynn and gotten their agreements in line, too. So by the time I grab my stuff, including my phone, a granola bar and my laptop, shove them in my backpack, kiss the folks, and fly down the stairs rather than pace, waiting for an elevator, Flynn was already here, leaning oh so casually against a car and of course chatting away with Detective Macdonald. I'm shocked he didn't Snapchat up a photo of the two of them for me to see.

Jimmy sees me pause and looks up, winks, and I hear him say, "Treppenwitz, Sid. Treppenwitz."

Treppenwitz, my friends, is German for "staircase joke" but what it really means is when you think of a witty, snarky comeback you should have said in the moment, but you didn't actually think of it until it's too late. You know, when you left the room and were heading down the stairs. Ever since it came up in a ninth-grade discussion about words that act as phrases, conveying an entire concept with just one word, Jimmy has used it to peremptorily punctuate my ability to think of perfect things right after the fact, whenever he can. Sometimes it's even funny. Sometimes.

But now is not one of those times. I just shut my mouth, grit my teeth, and glare at him. In return, he opens the car door for me with a big flourish all the while catching me up on the game plan. We have to go get Vikram, Ari, and Imani, but we will be splitting up to save some time. He and I will go with Tsarnowsky to round up Vikram while Emma goes to see about getting Ari and Imani.

As I am sure you can imagine, I would have loved to protest this as a sexist moment or something, but the truth is, Ari and Imani are included solely because we were all there last night, which put us all in this together today, because that's what friends do. And it's not like the extra bodies won't be of help. It is, however, Jimmy, Vikram, and me who are going to bring the depth of necessary skills.

So I bite back sharply on my tongue, belt in, and with that we head crosstown to Vikram's. And when we get there, it looks like his entire family is collected outside, smiling and waving to all of us. I mean there must be at least, I don't know, fifteen people milling around. And all the women are dressed up in these beautiful multicolored saris. It is equal parts spectacle and spectacular.

Tsarnowsky puts the car in park and gets out. We watch laughing, as he heads up toward the group, where his hand is being taken and repeatedly pumped by a man Jimmy and I guess has to be Mr. Patel.

So as Tsarnowsky chats for a moment, Vikram makes his escape, piling into the front seat of the car, turning to face me and Jimmy sitting in the back, this huge grin on his face, his thrill right out there. "This is like the best day of my life. My dad is so excited I am being asked to work with the police AND Jimmy Flynn on a project, it's like I won a Nobel Prize or something."

And go figure, Vikram is contagious. Jimmy and I whoop and start laughing hysterically, finally letting go of all our airs and defenses and flat out embracing our own giddiness.

Tsarnowsky extricates himself from the crowd, climbs in, looks at all of us, and grins. In this tale I tell, this may be the most key of all our moments I share. It is the moment co-conspirators are born. The moment the followers and the early adopters become one.

Tsarno turns over the key and as the car pulls away, we find ourselves consumed by an energy that turns nearly frantic as we wave back to Vikram's family, each one of us delirious in the moment. And in the midst of my delirium, I find the oddest clarity of thought; this Vikram really isn't such a loser.

EIGHT

We arrive at the station ahead of Detective Macdonald and her charges, where our pretty perky high continues, nearly making us skip our way down to the office of our detectives, but we don't. And I would tell you we exercised control because that's what we do, but honestly 1) skipping just so would not be cool and we are nothing if not concerned about being cool, and 2) we couldn't move faster than the Barno, who, let's be honest, wasn't in shape to set any land speed records. And on a personal aside, if I am honest, I truly did not want to risk speeding up and potentially banging into or tripping over something that could result in my touching anything, because I do not think they make enough hand sanitizer for this place, to serve and protect me. Which in turn, makes it just a bit hard for me to consider letting myself race along and throw caution to the wind.

And while I do realize this makes me sound like either a snob or a major germaphobe, I plead not guilty to both. I don't mind the grime and the grit of my city. I don't go to my fairly ancient school wearing a mask and gloves. But I will not stoop down to pick up the fries I accidentally drop on a sewer grate and then eat them. And even with all my adrenaline running around, I am just unable to shake feeling a little "sewer grate-y" here.

We walk past the bathrooms and as all three men decide to stop, I realize I am pretty much alone in my not-so-fresh-so-not-touching-that feeling.

But I survive the wait by avoiding both eye and wall contact.

It does occur to me as I look down I should have worn my boots rather than my sneakers. So much easier to hose off.

Upon their return, we set out at a much calmer pace and, as it happens, this momentary lull turns out to be a good thing. If I had kept on running on our collective high, I might have pulled up short and stumbled my way into touching something. But since I have no such head of steam, the door Tsarno holds open is perfectly safe, for my hands-in-my-pants, slow-moving-stance, to slither inside.

And thus not trip and fall forward onto my face. Because I am wrong, I am very wrong. It is not safe inside here at all.

The room is no bigger than a broom closet, necessitating the two desks to be positioned pushed to one wall, facing each other. I do not need too much brain power to figure out whose desk is whose. Her side, the one that faces the back wall, which means you could see the desk part as soon as the door swung open, has neat stacks of papers and pens of assorted colors and two large photos, one of a striking man and one of Goddess Emma Macdonald with the very same striking man and a big, happy, panting cocoa-colored "oodle." It stops me dead in my tracks. The other three push by me. My head is spinning and I can feel the bile in the back of my throat. My inner voice snaps to snarktention. "Of course they have an oodle. Of course."

Bile. Vile. Arrow to my heart launches. Direct hit scores. Launch raging fricking hormones. Tilt. Tilt. Flipper. Tilt.

And you know, even though I sort of knew sooner or later there would be something like this and I know I am being ridiculously, absurdly over the top, my internal emotional dramatic teenage hormonal self does not care. I mean I have plans. Okay, maybe they're not exactly plans, but they are darn good fantasies.

I, Sid Rubin, was going to strut my way in here today, solve this crime, and watch as Emma turned to me in awe. And to celebrate our accomplishment, I was going to take the now very grateful and very enamored Detective Goddess Emma Macdonald to a late picnic lunch, followed by Shakespeare in the

Park (for which I was going to camp out if I needed to so I could score tickets) and then after it ends we are going to walk through the Park, strolling our way through the Bethesda Terrace, sharing our awe at the Minton Tile Ceiling, and then, when we come out from the dark below and reach the open light of the Grand Terrace, I touch her back and guide her toward the fountain.

And as we approach, the fountain's twenty-six feet of highness rising majestically above us, I take her hand and tell her about how the bronze Angel that sits atop it is the only commissioned piece of art in the original park. And how Emma Stebbins, who sculpted her, was the first woman in New York City ever to be given that kind of commission. And how Emma Stebbins had gone to Rome to study art and came back with Charlotte Cushman, and they shared what was then called a 'Boston Marriage.' And the Angel is considered the embodiment of God and, thus by extension the embodiment of love. Which is why the Bethesda Fountain's other name is Angel of the Waters. And . . .

But before I can finish my next thought, Emma turns from gazing at the Angel's face, raises her hands to my lips, leans in, and we kiss.

OMG, Sid, change the freaking channel!

Slam. Back to the here and now as the picture mercifully vanishes from my eyes, swiped to the desk by the hand of Flynn.

Okay. Deep breath. I am back. I am going to ignore the tear that is threatening to unleash itself upon my left cheek and I am instead going to blink it back, look around the room, and get back to our case.

This doesn't appear at first glance to be a better plan. I exchange looks with Jimmy and Vikram who are also perusing the room and its antiquated contents. Wow. Revelry dies so quickly, the pall falleth fast. I can tell you none of my tax dollars, or at least my parents' tax dollars, are at work here.

"Um, Detective Tsarnowsky." Jimmy gamely steps into the void. "As we all have our own computers and such, maybe we could set up in a, hmmmm, larger room. No point really in cramming us all in here with your desktop."

Tsarno gives us all a slightly suspicious look, but it does lead to a grunt, followed by a "stay here, touch nothing," which of course, works for me.

And, you know, maybe we are all guilty of watching too much TV or something, but we are all looking around and not touching anything and, even more of a tell, not saying anything, almost as though we think the room is bugged. And I do realize I could be projecting here, that this is only my random paranoid thought, but I don't think so. It's sort of like we're all looking for the hidden camera. Like this is really a test and, oh way oh, they're watching us.

Before we get too carried away and start hearing *The Twilight Zone* theme, the door opens, heralding the noisy arrival of Imani, Ari, and Emma Macdonald, followed directly by Tsarno and, "Let's go."

¤ ¤ ¤

To where? Obvious answer: a conference room. Less obvious answer, given only in hindsight: "Through the looking glass, Sid."

But as with all hindsight opportunities, my friends, in the moment, we are only going down the hall, turning right and into a room done in cinder block with a large conference table. And no windows. And hard wooden chairs with four legs on the floor and no cushions. Perfect.

Backpacks pile on, gear piles out. Tsarno watches. I can't tell if that's admiration or horror on his face. "So what exactly are you doing?"

"Setting up a hotspot." Jimmy is incredibly good at not sounding superior. "Hey, Ari, can you hand Sid the cord over there, the one with the green band on it?"

"Why?"

As I said, Jimmy is a great diplomat. I was already struggling to not look at the suddenly unattainable Goddess, so I take over setup, which is really mostly about plugging into power and a few cords, but I do know how to make the simple look complicated.

"Well, if we use your internet connection, we're on the police station servers. And if we run across someone or something that might be helpful, the last thing we want is for someone to somehow trace us back to the police station servers. There's no reason to think they could, but if they could, I don't think it would be . . . prudent . . . for them to find us here." Jimmy pauses here, a quiet moment for Tsarnowsky to disagree if he's going to.

When nothing is forthcoming, Jimmy continues, "And I'm guessing you asked us to help you out because if you go to guys in the department you lose at least some control, not to mention at the very least you might have to explain us. So if we use our Wi-Fi, they won't know we're assisting you with this search. In a nutshell, Detective Tsarnowsky, our Wi-Fi gives us, and thus you, ultimate control."

You can see both Tsarnowsky and Emma weighing the explanation. Calculating us. And as they tally their risks, my attempt at ignoring my earlier overwhelming disappointment, however unfair that emotion might be, is given time and space to begin twisting itself into a bit of not-too-fair-either anger. And I don't care. I mean she has to know how I feel. I make the mistake of side-glancing up and over, and she is looking at me, and we all know that look, a little bit of sorrow, a little bit of pity. And I seethe and I want to whip at her, to make her feel my anger. To make her feel me. And I don't really care if it's irrational.

Double, double, toil and trouble. Itchy witchy, release my bitchy.

And with that, I take my best shot, smash right through Jimmy's lovely, grade school explanation, and start talking right above their heads. "We've got a custom firmware loaded on the hotspot." Overhead smash, right at you, Ms. Goddess. "This will take us for a ride, bouncing us around the world, masking each of our IPs using a few different VPNs," cross-court winner "which will lock down the ports for any unwanted traffic." Sweet fakey smile as I finish with a surprise dink, placing it so out of reach. Trust me, Emma Macdonald, way too much topspin for you.

And, now, freshly winded from my game, I stand here, not sure what to do next, when what I love the most about girlfriends, and I mean girls who are friends, not the dateable ones, springs into action. Girlfriends know when someone needs rescue, even if they don't know why.

Ari looks over to Imani, who immediately sidles right on up and quietly salvages the hotspot from my hands, returning it to Jimmy, who takes it and shows it to Tsarnowsky, while steering the conversation back to a, let's call it, more productive place, "What Sid is saying is this little baby is going to help us be a lot more discreet online with the added bonus of allowing us all to work from the same place without it appearing as though we are. So if we find something, it won't look like all of us were plugging in from the same room, but just random folks out and about on the online highway." And with that, Jimmy turns on our gizmo. "Okay. So what we're looking for is the LARP Tessa Sargentino would have been to, where it was held, and who threw it? Yes?"

As the detectives nod their agreement, Imani chimes in, "So. Finding a LARP is our first step. Easy enough. Right? Sid?"

All eyes on me. Apparently I am now the expert here.

Oh no. Incoming! Song Bomb! LARP for sale or rent. Bustier fifty cent.

Ignoring!

Focus, Sid. "Okay. I think off-hand we have a couple of options. We start by writing a script to search social media for LARP events in the city. For at least the bigger, more organized events, it will dump out raw information on who's attending, not attending, time, and location. Then, I think we cross-reference LARPS with the date. We'll be casting a wide net, so we'll still have to run through the data by hand. Lots of people are uncomfortable about coming, about being seen, especially at first, 'cause you know we're all just freaks who do this, etc., so there's always a lot of fake profiles and false information. And to confuse things even more, many LARPers will always keep their RPs."

Interruption. Detective Macdonald, "Their RPs?"

"Oh. Sorry. Their role-playing identities. So when they're online, they are always speaking in their character so they're giving away no real world information."

Emma nods her understanding and I continue. "If we can figure out what events were going on, we can likely find some photos from that day. A LARP in any semipublic place is bound to get not only their own people taking photos, but passersby as well. This might get us to a place to match LARPers who at least might have seen someone. Or maybe even, if we were incredibly lucky, a picture of Tessa with people we can track."

"Also," as I keep talking, my ideas keep expanding, "presuming it was kind of a usual LARP we can check with gaming stores, bookstores, and all those kinds of places to see if anyone put a listing on one of their boards or something. Maybe even small theaters, costume shops. I think we print out a list of those, and Imani and Ari can start calling around and checking."

Imani looks at me like a woman gone mad. "You do know there's a heck of a lot of stores in this city? Can we at least narrow down the area? You know, maybe check out Tribeca today, maybe the Village? I'm thinking that's a full day right there."

"Or maybe," Ari moves over perhaps a bit dangerously close to Tsarnowsky and smiles at me, "Imani and I should simply head out and go shopping for," her hands pushing her breasts in and up for emphasis, "period bustiers? Detective Tsarnowsky can come with us and flash his badge and pictures when we find a seller."

"Nice try, Ari." I've known her way too long to be shocked by her proposal, but she does make me laugh. "Put the girls away and," I do my best to look seriously stern, "tell them to behave. Look, there's all sorts of transportation in NY, so who knows where she would have been coming from. I mean she could have been killed during the LARP, but she also could have been heading home. Hell, she could even have been coming back from Jersey. I know there's a big space just over the line where they hold a pretty rad dystopian LARP."

And then, because I am experiencing a rather upside-down day (and given my run of them recently, it is perhaps my new normal, but I haven't conceded to such as of yet), surprisingly I am still not prepared for this other shocking event, which then unfolds. Vikram Patel not only speaks up; he has a good point. Astonishing, I know.

"I also think, maybe, Sid," Vikram approaches very carefully, "uhm, I don't think we should limit our search to LARPs alone. I mean, I think you are most probably right and, of course, she most probably was at a LARP, but I think maybe we should also check for masquerades or theater events, which could involve a costume. I think."

And as I am pondering the surprise of this moment, which apparently includes my mouth hanging open mid-sentence because I was all set to verbally poke him, I hear "Treppenwitz" from behind me. A bit off-target actually, but I'll take it. I do the guppy. Mouth close and mouth reopen. "Point taken. And specifically we should look for anything with Steampunk. I mean, to Vikram's point, maybe she was in a local play or teaching a class or something."

And with that we are off and running, or at least our fingers are. We are actually off and sitting.

¤ ¤ ¤

Although I don't know exactly what any of us exactly imagined, we are all proud members of the generation who believe we exist in an instantaneous universe filled with instant answers. We wait for nothing. It is always at our fingertips. I mean, dead chick in bustier? Isn't there an app for that?

And thus, I know we all imagined we would set up our grand search and, because we are all so brilliant and would have built such perfect hypotheses and parameters into our script, our neat little equation of code would spit out a timely answer, triumphantly proving us all to be the geniuses we imagine ourselves to be.

And that turned out to be as real as the rest of what I fantasized.

Instead, as the hours drag on and the reams of drab information keep piling up and nothing screams, "You-hoo!!! Here I am! I am Tessa Sargentino's killer! You have solved the case!" our morning high proves the axiom that what goes up must come down.

At five thirty we unplug, heading out the door, trudging our way home as promised, fatigued, deflated, leaving behind a tonnage of assorted paperwork for Tsarnowsky and (my now former Goddess) Emma, to follow up on. But the sad, not so hidden truth is, we all know our cache doesn't really add up to anything all that special.

NINE

Jimmy glances over to me, but I shake my head and he nods. In our unspoken world of friendship, he knows and respects I am not ready for company. He takes his big old arm, wraps it around Imani's shoulder. I watch her lean into him as the four of them turn away and head crosstown. I watch as they leave, a foursome, divided two by two. Then I head the other way, not willing, nor able, to return home yet. Home will have questions and I don't want to have answers. I don't even want to talk, about anything. To talk, I would have to force air past this lump in my throat and I am not ready to try.

So now, now I am alone. But not really. I am alone with my hurt, and with the lump in my throat, so I have plenty of pathetic companionship, which is not exactly alone.

And together we walk, me and my pathetic companions, heading to the High Line, trying to let the day get lost in the view, until finally I am chilled through, watching as the sun goes down and dark descends until then there is nothing else to see. And only then, there is nowhere else for me to go, except home.

And as I turn, there she is. The unattainable Detective Goddess Emma Macdonald. Standing there. Waiting. In the flesh. While I have big, puffy, yeah-I've-been-crying eyes.

Finally I nod and she joins me at the railing. We both turn and face out, looking over the city. I don't need to ask how she found me. Flynn would know where to send her.

I feel her turn toward me, but I don't move. She continues

studying me quietly and then breaks our silence. "Hey. I thought maybe you'd want to talk?"

I kind of look at her and shrug. I don't really know how to answer. It isn't about wanting to talk or not; truth is I'm not sure I have anything I can say. "Sorry. I was just hormonally wrong." It's all stupid teenage crush crap anyway.

"I am so sorry, Sid. I don't know what I thought. Or maybe I just didn't really think."

Maybe she doesn't know what she thought, but I know she thought I thought she hung the moon and the stars.

"Or maybe, Sid, I was just a bit flattered and a bit out of my league."

She tries the old nervous chuckle and a smile, but I am giving her nothing. I pull my jacket tighter, wrapping my arms around my chest. I gave her everything and she threw it away, so now she gets nothing. I do three years old great.

She takes a small step toward me, tilts her head to catch my eye. "His name is Carl. We're getting married in six weeks. He's a really great guy, and a really great cook." She smiles at me. "He's a Chef at Le Toque. I think you'd actually quite like him."

Again I say nothing, and after another minute of quiet, Emma turns back and joins me in staring outward, "I'd like us to be friends, Sid, but if that's not possible, I will ask if we can put this aside, because honestly Robert and I need your help to solve this."

Robert? My silent petulant moot vigil is suddenly interrupted, my FOMO kicking in, sending an urgent alert signal, an internal alarm telling me I have just missed something when I realize, duh, Robert is Detective Robert Tsarnowsky. False alarm.

Funny, I always think of her as Emma, or Goddess, but I only think of him as Tsarno or, well, as we all know by now, Tsarno Barno. It's odd how we attribute names to people. I mean some people are always formal and some people have instant nicknames and some people have a nickname and then it changes to another one and then to another one and . . .

I watch as Emma steps away from the rail, her hands smoothing her pants, swiping away some New York City grime. Squared-off, French manicured nails. I hadn't noticed them before. Suits her. Classic. Nice.

"So, can we make this work, Sid?"

In my brain, I hear the question repeat itself and I truculently answer myself, "I dunno." I bite the inside of my cheek, pressing my hands to my head. Big exhale. Hands clench hard around my rib cage. I attempt to look up, but it's still too soon. She looks just like Mary Stuart Masterson in the close-up when the tears roll down her cheeks and she first stole my heart. I took a screen shot of her in just that moment.

Finally, I meet her eyes; Emma is motionless, watching, waiting. The "can we?" question lies between us, caught "entre chien et loup," between dog and wolf, trapped in the twilight of our day, its howl echoing in the silence.

So I meet her eyes and nod. Kind of do that half-smile thing. Not because I want to, but because I can't think of anything else to do. And I can't stay here forever. And I can't let her down. It would ruin the already destroyed ending of my movie.

And with that, poof, she is gone. And it is time for me to grow up and go home. And when I get there, I find my prayer for no one else to be home just this once has become yet one more unanswered prayer in my day.

"Sid!"

Sheesh. Was he waiting on the inside of the door for me to turn the key? I force words through my mouth. "Hey Dad."

"Well, how did it go?"

Before I can answer, Mom has stepped out of the kitchen, slowly wiping her hands, stalling, waiting for me to answer the question so she might evaluate what she hears and only then choose her reaction to my late, okay, very late arrival.

I shrug off my backpack, turning to take off my jacket, letting me break eye contact. "Lots of stuff, but nothing real yet."

Mom chooses even-toned concern. "I kept a plate warm for you, Sidonie."

I shake my head, pleading not hungry and escaping to my

room. I put on my old, faded, chewed around the collar, shrunken peace-signed T-shirt and too short sweatpants, seeking them to comfort me like an old friend. And I sit and I wait, just quiet and sad.

First the gentle knock. Then the hushed, "Sidonie? Are you okay?"

And now my waiting is over. I was timing it, allowing for three minutes, but it takes only two and a half. "Oui, Mama. Just fine." We both know it's a lie, but it's mine to tell.

TEN

I don't remember falling asleep. I remember sadness and I remember tears. I remember reaching under my bed and pulling out my prized, first-edition collection of *Lumberjanes*, desperately wanting them somehow, for like the gazillionth time, to be real so I could run away and join them and Molly would share her magic bow with me and then somehow everything would be just fine.

I know I got under my blankets still fully dressed because I couldn't seem to get warm, but that's all I remember. I know I fell asleep because somewhere around three o'clock in the morning, I not only woke up, I bolted up, wide awake.

And I was restless, agitated.

So I try getting back to sleep. Try lying here in my bed, breathe in, breathe out, focus on staring up at the glow-in-the-dark constellations my Dad and I had pasted up so many years ago to keep me company when I went through a phase of waking up with nightmares. But trying to practice steady breathing isn't cutting it. No offense, Orion. My brain has a mind of its own.

It is time to get up and unleash the beast.

So in the dark of my room, I begin to think. If the LARP isn't coming to us, how do we get us to the LARP?

The obvious answer: go through Tessa Sargentino. If she was at a LARP I didn't know about and I couldn't find that LARP, how did she get there? I so badly want to get up and try to break into the police files to read through them, but even I know that's one really stupid idea. Even a bête belle Mama could not bail me out of that

65

fine fettle of kish as Dad likes to call what he considers my antics.

But there is another way. Forget the sleep. Wake up my body and wake up my computer.

Because you, Tessa, you are going to lead me to it. Step one. Introduce myself to you, Tessa; meet me, Sid, your soon to be new bestie.

We will become inseparable. I'm going to start our friendship by googling you, pulling up all the mentions and newspaper articles I can find. Ready, set, begin compiling. Let's see, ooh we have a nice notice from Argot Incorporated announcing your hiring. I'll just jot myself a note to check them out later. And here's an article you contributed to, discussing the rise of cryptocurrencies such as Bitcoin, Litecoin, and Peercoin. Wow, even a bit on Monero. Actually, some pretty interesting stuff in this one, Tess. I send it to myself so I can read it fully when I have more time.

This getting acquainted thing is kind of ridiculously easy, in at least that surface sense.

Link to your Facebook page. Sure. Click away. Loading. Loading. Wow. I don't understand how your Facebook page is 1) not yet memorialized, although perhaps no one knows to do it yet and 2) shockingly not private, although I am thrilled. I wonder if you even knew; maybe you missed their latest security settings update. However, via this happy happenstance, I can scroll through as well as link myself right into your Instagram account. So rather quickly, my list of, well, you is off and running.

Full name, Tessa Maria Sargentino. Confirmation name, Sulpice. Really? Sulpice. Eew. Wonder why you chose that? Age 32. Single. 5'7" tall, with brown hair and brown eyes. Born on 11 October in Brooklyn, NY. A Libra. Graduated Cum Laude from Hunter College. BS in Accounting. MBA Wharton's. Making a very good living at the previously noted Argot Incorporated, located in the new One World Trade Center Building. Big firm equals big apartment. Which apparently, for you, is in the spectacular Gehry Building at 8 Spruce. Wow. Sweet. And judging from the pics you posted, it looks like you are on the side overlooking the Brooklyn Bridge. Oooh, doubly sweet.

You have, or sadly you had, a cat. Sorry. Which you obviously think is a particularly exceptional specimen. Cat's name is . . . Fluffy. Really? Mr. Fluffy? You named a male cat Fluffy? And to think I was beginning to really like you. Oh. Ok. I see. Full name Mr. Fluffer-Nutter. Better. Kind of. Not necessarily great, but better. Oh, and here's a nice posting from your friend Greg. He's taken Mr. Fluffer-Nutter home and he's doing well. I give it a "like" for you.

"Oh shit." I suddenly realize how ridiculously casual I have become. "Hang on I can't be 'liking' things from your page. Dead people don't start liking things."

Okay. Fixed that. Continuing. Say three times, *I am Velma, I am not Scooby.*

Jinkies! Back to business. You wore braces. Also glasses, then contacts. You apparently had laser eye surgery recently and, from the looks of it, I'm guessing a nose job as well. Honestly can't say I blame you there. You know Tessa, upside down and pouring out of your outfit made you look a lot sexier than these pics. Obviously less animated, but sexier. Sorry. I know, probably not what you want to hear, and kinda sad, but true.

We have a mother named Theresa, father Carmine, and three older brothers. And. Wowzerhole. Daddy is a cop. And judging from all his shiny hardware, a pretty big one. And now all those little niggling thoughts I ignored because I wanted in make sense. Why come to a group of kids for help? It's not like Tsaro seems to delight in his interaction with us. And why would Emma offer to step away so I can help "Robert"? And really, why I got so hurt. It's because I felt played. Which I'm now thinking I kind of was. Played. Cause you know, it's all those little odd things you don't think about until the answer is in front of you and then you know. Because Tessa's not just another sad statistic of a girl murdered in the big city; Tessa's a police officer's daughter, which means it's personal, and if personal means they need a group of nerdy kids to break this case, then suck it up and go use them.

Okay. Now that I get that part, let's see what other questions I might not know I have until you give me answers.

It looks like you have one niece. Nona, your beloved Grand-mother, will turn ninety this year. Last year you took a trip to Spain. Seems like you traveled alone, but apparently made friends with your tour group. And five really good-looking guys in Barcelona. Sweet. The year before that looks like you went to Prague with three girlfriends.

No obvious boyfriend pics. Unlike, let's say, one Detective Emma Macdonald.

Just sayin'.

Gotta love a conversation with myself.

"Okay!" Shaking my head. "Enough." Okay, Sid, you got played. But only because you were playing! Focus!

Wow, talk about your doing well. Nice posting. "Just got a cut, color and Brazilian Blowout at M3." Jeez, the ungodly expensive, who's who of hip-in-the-city salon in Chelsea. Ow. Way to blow lots of hair and lots of money all in one trip! You go, girl.

Vintage purse. New York black trendy outfit. Manolo Blahnik shoes. Thank God you love to tag your stuff, cause it is so way over my head.

Food Pictures. I like a foodie. Wow. Don't know if you are a foodie or not, but damn girl, you like to eat out. A lot. Dragon Roll. Charcuterie. Ooohhhh, a Milk Bar cake. Sweet.

Apparently you are fond of Negronis. Blech.

Ooh. Nice pic here, Tess. From Yayoi Kusama's *Infinity Mirrored Room*. I will have you know I, too, have a picture from that. I went with Layla Sante. She was my very first girlfriend. She kind of looks a little bit like Archie Panjabi did when she was in *Bend it Like Beckham*. We were together for about three months, if I stretch and count pre-dating and hookups. So anyway, the two of us stood on line for like five hours to get in. It was such a grown-up date thing-y thing to do. When that show opened, taking a selfie in the Mirrored Room was the coolest, hippest thing you could do in NY. It was drizzling out and it was fricking freezing out and, in hindsight, pretty darn miserable, but I was so in love and didn't care. I was doing the coolest thing with the coolest girl in the coolest city.

Apparently cool is the word of the sleep deprived. Who knew? Coolest girl. Coolest thing. Argh. Vocabulary goes MIA in the night. I wonder if there's a syndrome for that. You know, Night Brain. I will cure myself. I will put my hands to my head. Give it a shake. Wake up, brain! You are cured!

Argh. Deep breath. Stop the run-on moronic-ness and tell her what you want, what you need, to know.

Tessa? If you can hear me, wherever you are, I need you to tell me who you went there with, who you went to the LARP with. Because I have to hand it to you, although I am getting bits and pieces of your life, absolutely nothing is saying, "I'm off to LARP this weekend." Nothing is even saying, "I LARP." Period. And I can't believe no one knows. Not possible.

I want to scream, "Where's the Steampunk!"

You—it, make no sense. Even if you only casually cosplay, something should be here, even a tiny detail of something. But there's nothing. Everything about you is on the surface shiny. It's all about your cat, your job, the bars and drinks with friends. But I know there's more. Because you know something, Tessa, I am so not going to accept for one moment that someone who could fill out a bustier like you did cannot fill out their life. That would be, that would be, well, wrong on a very basic level.

Ping.

Textus Interruptus. It's the Flynn. "A?"

"NMH" Not much here. So sadly true. "U?"

Before Jimmy can answer, I catch sight of the light gray dawn sneaking under the blind in my window, which startles me just long enough so I see my clock and realize I've been here for hours, like pretty much all night, and now, if I do not seriously haul ass, I am going to be late. And late will warrant an excuse from my parents. And an excuse from my parents will require an explanation. From me. Which I do not want to give.

Fluck!

Need to fly.

Now.

ELEVEN

Not only do I make it to school on time, I do it with seven minutes to spare. I also do it with breathing difficulties, which make me double over, allowing me to observe I have two different shoes on. Similar, mind you, but not quite the same. And just different enough that you know someone is going to notice. But not before I notice Jean, who is obviously sitting and watching for me, laughing as though my morning is his most entertaining program. Which, given that he has no life of his own, it probably is.

Before I can lunge and smack his stupid self upside his head for not waking me, even though 1) I was technically awake, just torpored and 2) I have told him a thousand times we do not buddy our way to school, Jimmy is racing over, using his angle advantage to cut me off. I do manage to yell "asshole" before my right arm is grabbed and spun away. But not before I see Jean stick out his tongue at me. There will be payback.

Jimmy drags me toward the left side of the steps where Vikram and Ari are hanging out, waiting. Imani, he lets me know, is running late. Whatever. It was just days ago she would have texted me such important information. But that was then and this is now. No time to form a pout; we have intel to share. As Jimmy and Vikram pull out their intel, Imani's lateness is forgotten history. We have only five minutes left before the bell, which turns out to be two minutes more than we need.

To summarize:

The sad news: we all pretty much have the same stuff, including

71

the big cop connection, but none of it getting us closer to what we need.

The happy news: we are all hooked!

The bad news: Jimmy is not available after school all week because there's no way he can miss practice. The coach will kill him. His parents will kill him. Blah. Blah. Blah. And if we are going to be honest about this, Five Fingers Flynn loves to play. He's the quarterback, the star quarterback. He's the guy who walks down the hall and people just want to reach out and high five, pat on the back, fist bump. He's not giving that up to research what LARP dead Tessa was attending. He is a man with priorities.

On the other hand, he isn't interested in missing out on any of this either. And thus, Four Fingers and a Thumb Flynn (that's my name for his left hand, as his right hand was what earned him the moniker Five Fingers Flynn) blithely suggests we could all meet at lunch and start digging some more.

Which is, of course, precisely what we do.

Noon. Library. Back corner. As far away from the steely eagle-eyed, gray-haired, polyester pantsuit-wearing Iron Lady of Libros, Battle-Axe of Books, Mrs. Stewart, not to mention any other prying eyes, as we can hope to get in this school.

We would be stealth personified if we weren't fraught with interruptions from classmates who either want us to shut up or want to know what we're up to with their "hey, how's it going" or "whazzup?"

In between our polite fake smiles, we go round and round, whispering loudly, shifting through our whole lot of nothingness, trying to somehow make nothing become something. Finally I can't take it anymore. "Look," I lean over and hiss, "Mr. Fluffer-Nutter is not the key and he's not going to be the key. We need Tsarno to get us her computer and her email password if they've got it."

Pause for the assembled mass as they inhale and ingest such a radical thought. Insert big morality question here. Well, big might be a bit of an exaggeration. We're kind of already programmed to get on with the getting on of this, but let's just acknowledge, in honor of Jimmy's rectitude (nice use of an SAT word, just noting for the record), he did take enough time to quickly hash through the implied morality behind the suggested action. If a person is dead, is reading their private correspondence and various profiles an act of hacking? Is it immoral for us to peruse their private correspondence?

Argue this in a series of mutters and hisses. Not easy, but actually kind of fun.

"Really," I hiss louder than the others, "think of us as Miep Gies and Otto Frank and this is *The Diary of Anne Frank*. Come on, do we honestly think Anne wrote her diary thinking one day I will publish my innermost thoughts and desires, and not only that, I will make it become required reading for strangers everywhere in the world? I'm thinking probably not. But for Otto and Miep and the rest of the world, having it published served a much higher cause."

So now they are all shutting up and looking at me. Good sign. Wait. Wait. I see it coming, and I raise a finger. Not your turn to speak, Flynn. I am going to address your objection before you can even say it. "And although I do not wish to stand, or sit, here accused of trivializing the significance of Anne's contribution," objection nicely overruled, "I think the point to be made is serving the higher cause. If we can pore over Tessa's writings and determine who killed her and why, her writings will have served that higher cause. The higher cause of justice."

"And, not only that," like a tennis return, all heads swing over to Vikram. "It is even a scientifically reasoned request," he says, a small grin creeping out across his face.

I know I am not the only one puzzled here.

"Occam's Razor," is all Vikram says, pushing back from the table, his palms lifting up to say, "what else could it be?" as perfunctorily as if he said it.

I start laughing as does Jimmy—Ari and Imani, not so much.

"Old medieval principle," Vikram explains while Jimmy and I continue to laugh, "which can be summed up as the simplest answer is most often correct."

"Occam's Razor, huh?" Ari smiles, leans into Vikram, and plants quite the kiss (and I mean, quite the kiss, as I'm still surprised they are both still breathing) on, in, up, down, and around his mouth. Finally surfacing for air, Ari turns back to the rather squirmy remnants of us. "We," apparently referencing herself and Imani, "just call it KISS. As in, Keep It Simple Stupid."

Oh yeah. Treppenwitz, Rubin. Treppenwitz. See I don't always need Jimmy to point out my obvious. Sometimes I can just remind myself.

¤ ¤ ¤

So, there are several prizes that come from being right and one of them, who knew, is winning the who-gets-to-call-Tsarno-the-Barno-sweepstakes and convince him to get us her cell phone, computer, and whatever access they have managed to gain. Which is how I came to be standing outside of Tsarno's favorite dumpy diner, waiting for him to show.

When I initially called him, which would have been right after Ari sat back down and let my blood pressure return to normal, he just said to meet him here after school let out. I don't know if he's coming with Emma or not and I don't know which way I want it to be. So I try to stand here being indifferent, but that's kind of not happening, so mostly I hang out near the street side of the entrance and pace. As I arrived thirty minutes early, I can tell you it is eight paces between the alley and the street, and six paces across. There is a slight uneven meeting of two slabs of cement, which could create a nice tripping point if one paid no attention to where one was going. Not a problem for one who is hyper-focused upon one's feet.

However, I decide to stop pacing and look up, as right now I can entertain myself by watching the meter cop come down the street and write tickets, waiting for the minute someone comes out to scream. It's always a losing game, but generally a cheap thrill to watch. Every now and then you get either a real whack job or someone who just starts sobbing and it truly does seem to be the end of their world. Either extreme kind of spoils the fun.

One time, when I was on eighth avenue heading home ...

Never mind. Sorry. Gotta save that one for another time when Tsarno's not getting out of his car, hitching up his pants.

I look carefully from my perch in the alley. He's alone. I still don't know if that makes me sad or relieved. I guess it's a little bit of both.

Tsarno rolls and waddles his way down to me, half grunts hello and this time as we make our way back to the booth, I nod hello to "our" waitress and ask if I can get a coffee. Tsarno motions for two as we sit down. Then he looks at me, waiting.

Okay. I can do this. I will cut to the chase. Inhale. Wipe palms on legs. Exhale. "We need her computer. We spent last night and today at lunch going through the stuff we could access without trying to actually hack her accounts and there's nothing in there."

I will share with you, Tsarno is looking rather, hmmmm, I shall pick the word "askance," at me. Askance, as in he is looking at me with eyes and a face filled with mistrust. I prefer that thought to the other option of he's looking at me as though I have lost what's left of my rational mind. Or even, he's looking at me as if I just grew three heads and, poof, I am now a three-headed dog named Fluffy (yes, a fair and square HP reference). Although come to think of it, it would actually be hysterical if that was how Tsarno was seeing me, because I just can't imagine him knowing that reference. But then again, if you think about it, there is something a bit Hagrid-ish about him. True, a lot shorter. But still somewhat Hagrid-ish. Maybe we could call him Hagrid light?

Clink. The lovely sound of coffee cups jostling, announcing their arrival, mercifully stops my internal ramblings.

Instead I watch, half fascinated and half horrified as Barno leans over and paws the white sugar packet holder, emerging with a fistful. He then puts four sugars in. Blech. Now he reaches for the cream. Wow. I mean really, what's the point? Why not just order an éclair from the display case in the front?

Okay. Take a minute. Sip my coffee, black, for the record. Nice civilized moment and go, jumping back in. "Look, forgetting whatever the legality is here for just a minute," nice eye pop, Tsarno, "even if we were to try hacking into things like her LinkedIn account, all that's gonna happen is three tries and they will seal the account."

I realize I am either sounding desperate or this coffee has an unusually large amount of caffeine. I hear the falsetto hit my brain. Sing with me, "speed talking, la la la la la." Slow it down. Get a grip. "Take her Facebook account. Today we can read her postings, but someone, someone is going to tell them she's dead and they will memorialize it and then we won't be able to get in, because even right now, even though I can get onto her page to read it, I can't confirm our friendship. So once it's sealed off, we're out."

I come up for air. He's still just staring.

OMG. I once again bow at the altar of the great, and prolific, Robert A. Heinlein who once wrote of trying to teach a pig to sing, "It wastes your time and annoys the pig." He is so right. I am doomed.

"The important thing here," I bravely continue in my attempt to find an oink we can share, " is we know it's somewhere in her system and we just need to find it. Tessa didn't go out to a soiree dressed like that without there being some, I don't know, invitation. And if she's posting every freaking meal she eats out, where's *that* post? It makes no sense."

Tsarno snorts. This seems to be working. He leans forward while he signals for the bill. Kind of gets right up to my eyeball. "You and Detective Macdonald are okay?"

Gulp. "Yeah. Sure. Why?"

"Because I don't really understand a damn thing you've said, but I get the gist. And Emma knows the guys who currently have all the computer paraphernalia you want." He reaches down, comes back with his money clip, throws a few bills on the table. "Looks like I'm stuck with you both." And then he smiles. Nicely.

"Saturday, three o'clock outside at the station." I am guessing my poker face wasn't working and he could see how shocked I felt, because he continued, "I know. Sounds like a long way away. But it's not. Look, Sid, if we get lucky and solve it today, ah well, I'll still have appreciated the help. But you know what, the statistics don't lie. The more time away from the crime, the tougher it becomes and trust me, none of this is going anywhere. You got any idea how many cases those guys in the evidence room are trying to get processed on any given day?"

Given what we know about Tessa that Tsarno doesn't know we know, not the answer I am expecting.

"Hey, I pull you in after school, your parents are gonna kill me. Besides, where's the rest of your posse?"

I know it's not exactly a redundant question, just a fisher. Still, I mentally check off the answer: football, chess club, singing lesson, and one more, which I don't actually know. Out loud, I choose the more pointed and yet self-deprecatingly droll "Short straw."

But make no mistake; I am still not happy nor mollified.

TWELVE

Time for another simple pop quiz question. Do you know what you call three brilliant minds gathered round a computer getting absolutely nowhere?

A Geek Tragedy.

Ba Dum Bum. Tish! Okay. Stop moaning and groaning. It's kind of funny. If not laugh out loud, it is at least titterable.

So, as you can tell, we did manage to "hang in there" and make it to Saturday. Barely. I think I personally memorized every single picture Tessa Sargentino has ever posted, or been tagged in, on FB and Instagram. I could probably walk into her office building and say hi to at least half the employees using their first names.

Which really might not be a bad plan.

And I think this why?

Because I now know a bad plan when I think it. You see, I have already been to her apartment building to "investigate." I have chatted with the doorman, got nothing. I tried a stake out approach but there is no "street view" to see and most people aren't inclined to stop and chat with a random teenager they are sure is out to hustle them for something. Which I guess I am, but obviously not the hustle they are all so worried about. And yes, I did wear a decent outfit.

So anyway, after I launched my underwhelming stealth attack, I realized even if someone were inclined to share an odd moment of chatty warmth, the odds of my newfound chattiér (fake French chatty friend) actually knowing Tessa would be slim. The Gehry building has like a thousand apartments. Which don't even start until after the first five floors, which is a school.

And let me just point out, none of this is ever an issue in a cop movie. But then again, neither is parking. And there's not a New Yorker alive who doesn't know that's a joke.

So, we can now surmise, some people are born gumshoes and some people, after eight hours of nothing to show, are born gumshoeless.

But now that I am thinking of it, Tessa's office peeps would be a way easier target. I mean I'd already have all these talking points to begin with. And if I do it on a day Imani's available, she's the most amazing person at starting conversations with brand-new people because, as she says, she's been doing it her whole life.

I'm liking this idea. Could be a genius opportunity.

But not today.

And as always, I thank you for asking . . . because today is finally Saturday and we are spending it back in the wonderful world of cinderblock, all booted up, all hovering one over the other, all of us salivating to get at this. And all of us, as we are discovering, are sadly all dressed up with no place to go.

In spite of Emma having delivered. We have Tessa's computer and login info; we're into her gmail account, which so far has revealed nothing. And I mean pretty much nothing. Zero. Zilch. About the only thing I can claim to have learned is that reading someone else's email is by and large pretty freaking boring. Okay, and yes, we found her passwords for LinkedIn, her invitation to join Sparkology, and a bunch of other business and social media sites, but nothing is taking us anywhere we need to go.

I can tell you Tessa hates her boss. Thinks he's an idiot. And her newest client, she is pretty sure, has cooked the books. Maybe she should lose him? But then again, he's worth a lot of billable hours. Lovely.

I can also tell you she and Michael Z in the office had a hot affair for about three months, six months ago. And that might have been something except Tsarno and Emma already knew about him and he already alibied out, so our little mini-jolt of joy was quickly snuffed out.

According to her browser history, she is on the hunt for a new microwave. She follows vegetarian recipes on Flipboard, which is only interesting because her food shots tell a very different story. Orders online from her Amazon Prime account all the time. She is planning to see Billy Joel at his Madison Square Garden gig. A whole lot of no there there.

And Imani and Ari aren't faring any better. They are still calling all over New York and no one seems to know anything—or at least if they do, no one is talking.

By the end of our session, we have nothing. Not even our belief in my assumption. It's a long walk home.

¤ ¤ ¤

Bolting awake. Again. Three in the morning. Again. Only this time, I have it! I know the answer. Chat rooms. We need to find it through chat rooms. However this LARP came about, someone has to know about it in order to go to it and somewhere there has to be a chat room for it.

¤ ¤ ¤

"No. I am telling you we approached it all wrong." I pleaded, begged and frankly just plain bullied everyone into canceling their plans and regrouping back at Platitude. Well, almost everyone. Emma is somewhere working her magic to try and bring the computer back. "We're searching her computer hoping to find *the* connection. You know, that person she was emailing with or that letter she wrote or even that bustier she ordered online from, I don't know, Bustiers are Us. It's not going to be there." I pause for just a second, checking that I have everyone's attention.

"She's using a hidden chat room. We need to look for IRC Channels or maybe Jabber Chat or who knows, even ICQ. We need to find that application."

81

For a moment everyone is frozen, mulling, thinking, assessing. Then The Flynn nods, not only in agreement, but in impressivement and I feel my self-worth smug up as the excitement begins to regenerate. And while it may not be nice to allow my smugness to rise, yesterday I had taken quite a beating. I mean no one said anything, but we all know the LARP was my conceit and it was bombing out in a big way. So I am going to smug this for all it's worth.

"Yeah?" Detective Tsarnowsky on the phone cut in on my glorious gloat. We all watch and wait. "Great. See you in ten." He hangs up, turning his focus back to us. "She's got it. Let's go."

¤ ¤ ¤

We get back and get down to business. This time, Jimmy, Vikram, and I take time to clone the computer onto ours so rather than leaning over each other's shoulders we can quadrant the system and section out work areas.

This efficiency, by the way, cost us about fifteen minutes of time while we shared an explanation of the process with Emma and Tsarno. "We are not changing anything in Tessa's computer. We're just making an exact copy of her system, which allows us to explore all the data without touching or compromising the original."

Apparently Emma had had to swear to her pals we would "only be looking," and "we wouldn't change anything," and she had to toss in a bit of begging and promises of coffee for the upcoming week. So as she saw our cables and cords being pulled from here and there, and heard words like "brute force rooting access" being bandied about, well, she got a little, we'll just call it wiggy. Telling her to chill didn't seem like a very prudent plan, so Vikram and I took a minute to pause and conquer. Which was working.

"We will run our versions through the usual VPN and such to mask our use, in case we stumble upon something where a dead person typing would be technically a big giveaway. And by setting ourselves up this way we can all take sections and be working on the problem simultaneously."

I smile at Emma with what I hope translates to calm and assured, "Frankly, we are just becoming a hub of virtual, stand-alone Tessa Sargentino machines."

And so we were. Well, more or less. Imani and Ari did go out and grab a bunch of chips and assorted colored waters to keep our energy up.

"Damn, Sid. You were right! She's using ICQ. The program is in here and," Flynn is yelling out from where he's working, his fingers flying across the keys, "it's in the E directory. The folder is labeled XXXOXOXXX, which is why we didn't catch it. And she must have a gadzillion saved chats. Wow."

"ICQ?" Blow me the fuck away. Oops. Pardon my language. But ICQ? I mean I know I was the one who suggested it, but I only tacked it onto my list so my thinking would look bigger and more impressive. I never actually thought it could really be an answer. Without getting too complicated, ICQ is really old. It was developed sometime in the '90s, I think. It's binary and text only.

But there it is, and here we are. We all immediately access Tessa's file, and Jimmy's right; there are tons of saved messages. And all of them are recoded to display in a series of x's and o's. So anyone casually looking would not necessarily twig to what is there. But who would even be looking? This whole ICQ thing is just weird. So now, in order for us to read them, we first have to change them over to ones and zeroes, which we then have to convert from binary to text.

Vikram takes the lead on this, and as the first half-dozen or so convert into plain English, my oh my, the things we are learning about our Ms. Tessa Sargentino and why she 1) keeps so many records and 2) keeps them so private.

Because was I so right. Tessa likes to chat. A lot. And while she kept her public profile all sweet and chatty about her cat and her food, her ICQ chat was a lot more, hmmmmm, interesting.

First of all, as I said, she was chatting using a program, which was not exactly what, or where, anyone would have any reason to go looking for her. But we did go there. And we did find her. But only sort of.

It turns out, in ICQ land, Tessa Sargentino is known as Mistress Philomena. And judging from her conversations, Mistress Philomena likes to chat about . . . Well, wow, my face flushes. This is way harder than I thought. I'm just going to put it out here before I chicken out. Mistress Philomena likes to talk dirty. And I mean seriously, really dirty. As in words I don't even know and words I don't want to hear being read aloud, particularly when sitting around with a group of your pals and buddies. No. No no no no no. You know, sitting around talking dead bodies is one thing. Talking hips and clips and, oh, all kinds of whips, entirely something else.

A case of major ick seeps over our crowd, causing us to sit here and try to avoid all eye contact, as we grind to an uncomfortable and, well, mortifying halt. Dead silence. Live awkwardness. Wow. And Tsarno's going to have to tell her father and brothers. Ew.

"Okay, people." Almost as though he could hear us, Tsarno clears his throat, snaps his fingers in front of Vikram's face to get his attention off the screen, "Let's not make it like you haven't read these words before."

And if I'm going to maintain my honest streak, I have to fess up. Some of them I never have. And I have a pretty darn impressive vocabulary. I'm sure most of them I could figure out with the old context clues trick, but right now I don't have the time.

Because I find I am now trapped in a bigger problem, a kind of hoisting with my own petard as Shakespeare, or Ms. James, our rather annoyingly nasal eighth-grade English teacher, might have said. Given this extraordinary discovery of Tessa's double life, Tsarno and Emma are rapidly shifting the focus by having everybody stop everything else to convert and print every Mistress Philomena chat, because they are now thinking it's "John Gone Bad" or "Tricked" or some other poorly pornographically titled chapter of Tessa's life, whose plot can be summarized as, when working as a call girl, it all went wrong.

And I cannot argue this. It is a very plausible theory. One, which for the record, does explain how she affords her apartment, food, and hair. But I still believe it's not the answer. From the moment I saw her I knew she was LARPing and I still believe the answer is a LARP. And now, I am once again all alone.

But maybe I'm not all alone. Maybe it's both. Maybe the LARP was a date with one of these chatty guys? Maybe she was out LARPing and one of these guys saw her and killed her?

"Argh!" The room turns to look at me, which is a bit embarrassing as I have my face smushed between my hands. Apparently I was using my outside voice with fist pound accompaniment. Who knew? I remove my hands, free my face, and give one of those "sorry" shrugs, while rolling my eyes and snarling to myself. I try to recover by chomping a handful of chips and looking back down at my screen.

And as Ari and Imani scoot their way over to team up with Vikram for converting/sorting/printing detail and Jimmy continues making his way through the E drive seeking more, I casually slip my online cloned Tessa files away from the ICQ crowd and imagine she and I reboot all the way back to the beginning.

THIRTEEN

Inhale. Exhale.

Focus on the screen. Pretend the screen is dark. I am Tessa. I come home. I boot up my computer and I go somewhere to look for my, I don't know, maybe my invitation or my instructions, or something. I don't bother with my email because I know it won't be there. I check my calendar, but there is nothing.

Okay. Start again.

I am Tessa. I come home. I boot up my computer and go off to change my clothes. I come back. I sit down. Maybe I've stopped and poured a glass of wine. A nice pinot gris. I take a sip as I flip through my phone book, looking for, not a name, not a number, but a something, anything to make contact. Maybe it's a nickname. Or a code. Or a line from a song. Something that just doesn't fit. I find nothing.

"Stay with us, Sid." I give myself my own personal pep talk. This is no time to let frustration rule myself. Breathe deep. Focus. Start again.

I am Tessa. I come home. I toss down my bag, I boot up my computer. I've waited all day. I want to get to it. Fast. Come On. Load. Load. It's got to have easy access. So I . . . Don't think, Sid; you're Tessa, just do it. So I pop open . . . Launchpad and, my fingers circle the air, eenie meenie miney mo. I pick, my eyes and fingers line up, click Dashboard. Really? Dashboard? Who uses their Dashboard?

Holy Shit. Apparently Tessa Maria Sargentino does. Whoa. Because here it is. In plain sight. On a hot pink widget Stickie. Jinkies, Velma! Pay dirt.

FOURTEEN

"Hey Jimmy?" I whisper, kind of loudly, urgently. He looks up and I motion him over with my head. I point to the Dashboard Stickie in front of me. "Is that what I think it is?"

Jimmy leans over my shoulder and then he leans in further, "Shit, Sid."

I nod, not turning around. "Jinkies, Flynn." I raise up my fist and he bumps it, both of us still staring at the screen. It's intense and we're being very quiet, but it doesn't matter. Everyone in the room has stopped and looked over. And it's this absolute sudden silence, which creeps its way up from my neck until it permeates my consciousness, breaking my focus, which in turn breaks Jimmy's, and so we turn to look at them, looking at us, and then we look back at each other.

It's Tsarno who interrupts the moment, barking, "What? What is it?"

And it is Emma, who has snuck up behind Jimmy to see what caused our sidebar, who answers. "It's a web address." She looks up at Tsarno, raising her eyebrows, then turns to me for maybe clarification, maybe confirmation.

"Well yes and no." I answer the unasked but implied question while I keep staring at the Stickie, mesmerized by the unique address with its telltale symbols. I break uneasily into a more detailed explanation. "It's a Tor address. She has a copy of Tor loaded somewhere in her system."

Before I finish, Vikram is out of his seat and confirming for himself what I have said. Ari watches him race over, looks to

Imani who shrugs her own lack of understanding, and God bless her, Ari gives our resident luddite Tsarno Barno a break by standing up and hollering, "Great. That's just great. I mean really fabulous. I'm sure." And as we all look up at her exaggerated antics, she continues, "Sid? Vik? Do you mind telling the rest of us? What the fuck is a Tor?"

"Tor is a web browser. Like Google Chrome or Firefox or Safari. Only it's totally anonymous to all the parties." Jimmy and I both listen as Vikram is doing a fine job both placating and explaining. "Meaning you can't trace the posting party and they can't trace you."

I decide it's time to get helpful, before Vikram can have all the fun. "You probably actually know Tor by its more common nickname . . ." I trail off and milk the building anticipation for just a second. I've earned a bit of dramatic effect. And then I drop my voice and, wait for it, the bomb. "The Dark Web." If this were a crime of the week and we were the high-tech cadre of feared, secretive injustice fighters, now would be a great time for a fabulous ominous music cue as we fade to black.

But instead of triumph, we come back from our commercial break, during which time Sultry Sid and her ace and mostly trusted sidekick, Foxy Flynn have made off-camera moves which would indicate they are going to take this info and copy, paste and click their way fearlessly into the internet highway of doom. However, before they can hit the paste button and carry out their mission to rid the world of yet another toxic villain, one of their own is hit with a case of the jitters. Yes, I am speaking of the dreadful losing-of-one's-nerve disease.

"I don't know, people, maybe it's not a good idea for us to be, go, here or there, or wherever."

Oh no, Tsarno. Now you're going to try and bring reason to this? Tune in for our all-new episode of Tsarno the Barno is *Scared Straight*. I don't think so. We did not do all this digging so we could turn it over and miss out on the best part. I start to mentally force myself to ignore my rising panic and memorize the web address.

Because I am so going there—with or without the Barno.

"Detective Tsarnowsky." As always, it's the Flynn to the rescue. Pulse-settling, nerve-soothing Flynn. "It's okay. It's oddly even safer for us than the other searches we were doing. As Sid was explaining, because Tor is based on anonymity, this setup is actually better for us. They won't know us, which makes surfing for answers a lot easier." Jimmy pauses, waiting for Tsarno to give us one of his patented snorts. Not so much. Jimmy shrugs a bit and continues, "Of course, the challenge is, when we find something, we won't know them either."

Detective Macdonald laughs at that. "You know, every perfect plan has an equally perfect fatal flaw."

And as she and Detective Robert Tsarnowsky exchange looks, he nods his resigned agreement and everyone begins to crowd around my screen and me. But before I hit any buttons, click any keys, I lean back in my chair. And maybe I am smirking just a bit. Remember, it was just this morning I had to plead and beg to get them here. So if there's a wee bit of gloat to be had, I am so having it. "Hey you know, I'm thinking, maybe we should wait. You know, regroup and come back, oh, maybe next Saturday at, oh I don't know, three o'clock?"

"Hey Sid?" Imani ducks under Jimmy's arm so she too can see. "Yeah?"

First comes the shoulder push, followed by, "Shut up and click."

And you know, for the first time since she and Jimmy began dating, I am so happy she's still Imani and we are just us. So I listen and do just that. And we're off. Flying down the rabbit hole of the dark web to find the freaking LARP.

As I'd never been on a Tor site before, I am imagining I will head into a smoke-filled screen and everything will be dark and ominous. What I get is kind of underwhelming. It's a scroll. It has a fancy seal, which kind of looks like an eye and reads:

Beware all who enter here.

Suddenly the seal turns and breaks apart, allowing the scroll to, well, open up like an old-fashioned pirate map thing-y:

If you do not come
to play your part,
Leave this stage
to those with heart.
For only those
Who will die for their art
Are welcome here
In the Third Eye of Sartre

Wow. Apparently we are chasing an Existentialist Poetic, using that term loosely, who LARPs. Go know? Before any of us can decide what to make of this, the scroll rescrolls and another sealed scroll appears. Same eye, different message.

Information is Not Free.

Okay. Think, Sid. You know Tessa. My hands beat a rhythm as I stare dead on at my computer. Got it. Tessa knows cryptocurrency. "Bitcoins. There must be some kind of account. We need to find her Bitcoin info."

"I'm on it." Jimmy leaps over to one of the other clone screens, furiously scrolling and typing away. "Got it, got it. She was using an exchange. Put in this number."

Pulse jumping. Entering. Shit. "Need to know how much to send. Is there any kind of record?"

"I've got something. Looks like two days before she died she moved one coin."

"One?" I hear the echo of Ari asking the same. I know we are both kind of shocked, but not for the same reason. I am asking the question of Jimmy, knowing I am only seeking confirmation. I am guessing it's value could be anywhere between a low of $300 and a high of maybe a thousand, maybe even a bit more. It's not my specialty, but I do know the asking price for Bitcoins keeps jumping around. But the point is, high or low, it's still a shitload of money for a LARP.

I can hear a murmur in the background and I realize Vikram is quietly explaining Bitcoins aren't dollars, so a one is not so cheap.

Jimmy's face is as unsure as mine, so I take my thinking out and socialize it. "I say let's go with the one coin and hope if it's too low, the program will just demand more, and if it's too high, more than we need, maybe it somehow credits the account back, so we won't look like idiots. Yes?"

Almost everyone around the table nods. Even though I am itching to get through this, I wait for Tsarno. He looks unbelievably uncomfortable. I'm kind of feeling bad for him. Here he is, stuck for hours in a room with people speaking a foreign language and he has to trust in it. He looks at me in that way people do who are impressed, all while wondering if I am an alien. "Go for it, Sid," he snorts, shaking his head. "Offer a one."

So I do, and as we all collectively hold our breath, the seal breaks, the scroll unfurls.

> Who are you and what role have you to play?
> Choose wisely if you wish to stay.

All eyes back on me. "Okay." I look quickly around the room, calculating. I see Imani's hot orange-cased phone on the other end of the table. Perfect. Wi-Fi not hooked into our setup. "Imani. Get your phone, go up on your regular web browser, and use it to find a Steampunk name generator site and get me a random name. Make sure it's female. And hurry. I have no idea how long we can sit in this window."

"Sid, what if this time it's not a Steampunk LARP?" Jimmy's voice is cracking as it tries to handle his adrenaline, "What if this time it's dystopian play?"

Imani's thumbs fly, not waiting for me to sort this out. "How's Marchioness Winnie Barrowcliffe-Bantam?"

"Great. And it's marchioness as in Martian-ness not march-ee-o-ness. A woman who is a marquis is a marchioness." I know that correcting Imani is not cool, but it's part knee jerk reaction and even part-er a result of my feeling the pressure of this and trying not to panic.

And I'm also stalling because I have to still answer Jimmy. "If whoever wrote this didn't specifically say it's something else, it would be the same. The steampunk is the connection to how it got started."

Deep breath and I type.

I am Marchioness Winnie Barrowcliffe-Bantam and I am a Rakeshame.

Ari has taken Imani's vacated spot and she leans over me in her "too close for comfort" way and reads as I type. "A what?"

"A vile, dissolute wretch. Archaic." I hit enter. "It's one of my favorite words."

"Of course it is." Ari leans in close to my ear, whispers. "You are so weird." And then, she licks it! My ear that is. I squirm, jump, and swat all at once while she bursts out laughing. As I turn to glare, she points back wildly.

A blank scroll has appeared and type is filling in across the middle.

Welcome Rakeshame.
See You There.
If You Dare.

And up it scrolls until it seals itself. And as it scrolls up, the invitation, which was hiding under it, is revealed.

Death is Immurement
A LARP in Three Acts
Will You Be The Chosen One
It's eight pm for those who would star
The rest of you come watch from afar.
Solve the Riddle
Be On Time
If not, oh well,
Tis the End of the Line
Your Password to Higher Learning
The World is Quiet Here

The screen goes black, leaving us all staring, until an annoyed Ari breaks the silence, "Jesus guys, 'Death is Immurement,' really?" Ari's miffed-ness is not surprisingly rather exaggerated. "Immurement, Imminent." Her hands gesture palm up, palm down and now, yep, they toss up to the wind, "Talk about asshole can't spell."

"Oh no, Ari." I follow the air her hands have left behind up and over to Jimmy, still at the other computer. "You're very wrong. Asshole can spell." I am speaking, but slowly, trying to piece together what I can't believe is true even as my mind races a million miles a minute knowing it is. "An immurement is building somebody into a wall. Very Edgar Allan Poe, 'Cask of Amontillado.'" I pause to look around, stopping at Detective Tsarnowsky. I take comfort in seeing him there. His bulk is actually reassuring. "You see, I think he, or she, isn't misspelling. I think they are actually announcing in their invitation, what their plan of death is. Death is Immurement. I mean it's kind of genius. Sick. But genius."

FIFTEEN

The next few hours are kind of an exhilarating blur. First of all, I am not only right. I am so right. And I absolutely love being right. Especially when no one believed me. So I am flying higher than a kite and my brain is zipping left and zagging right, zip-zag-zip-zag, and I know if I could show it to you, it would look like some visual effect designed for *Tron* or something.

"Um, Sid?" Imani nudges me from behind. "We do have a dead person here, you know."

Okay, so maybe my giddiness is a little inappropriate for the situation. I shall now sober myself up. I snort. Or not.

Emma Macdonald chooses to ignore my not-so-stifled self and gets us back to business. "If this is right, we theoretically know what's going to happen next. There will be a victim and that person will be buried in a wall. But that's only if this is right. How do we know that this person is the killer of Tessa Sargentino?" And as she speaks, she rotates about until she is facing me. "If being a whack job were the only requirement for becoming a murderer, none of us would be allowed on the streets."

Pointed comment or just luck of where her feet stopped? Hmmmm.

But I do get her question. Which means thinking deeper and musing aloud: "Okay, somehow he gets this link out and that's how you get in. And you only see the one upcoming game. Nothing ahead. Nothing behind. So without more, we can't actually say if this is the first LARP and just coincidence, or if this is the tenth and there are tons of victims. Because the problem is, at its core, Tor is designed to keep everything hidden from sight. Hence, the whole "dark web" thing. There is no search engine."

I pause trying to let everyone, mostly Tsarno and Emma, catch up. "Okay. So if you go up to Google and you type, let's say marijuana, you would get a definition from Wikipedia and articles on the history of and the fight for legalization and recipes for, I don't know, making banana bread pot pudding. On Tor if it were a search engine, you would get, let's say, oodles of places to shop and buy. You'd even have sites to let you compare prices and get coupons. But it's not. So you don't. You need to have a point of entry, a kind of passcode, for what you want. So we can get "here," but there's no road to any "there.""

Unfortunately, that not only summed up our problem way too well, it was what you might call a mood killer. It was not a good note to leave on, but it was time to go.

¤ ¤ ¤

And I would love to report to all of you the following:

It's three o'clock in the morning. Again. I bolt awake. Again. And I have a genius idea. Again.

But I can't, because I didn't. This time the tale has a few small differences. It's three o'clock in the morning. I am sound asleep. On my keyboard. We are both crashed. Exhausted. I am rudely jolted awake by the Jimmy/Sid early warning emergency system.

Yes, it would be more timely and efficient if we could just Skype or Facetime each other, but the issue is parents. Actually, to be more precise, the answer is parents with excellent hearing. You see, we can hide cell phone light and computer light under tents made of blankets and such, but if we start to talk out loud, all could be discovered.

So as I sit up and start to type, I use the bottom corner of my T-shirt to wipe the drool off my mouth and keyboard. Gross. Decoding. "Where the hell am I" and "check my email NOW."

So I do. There is an email from Vikram and with it are two attachments. They are both partial screen shots. The background is a moon, slightly past full, with dark type, the first of which reads:

At the Time of the Wanion
A New Necropolis Is Upon Us.

The second of which is:

Who Will Be The First
To Hallow Our Ground
With Body and Soul
So Forever We Are Bound
Welcome to
A LARP In Three Parts

And although details are missing, there is no question what Vikram has found.

And my brain neurons runneth over with a kaleidoscope of traffic. The most prominent seem to be 1) Holy Heck, Sidman, Vikram did it! 2) Where in Tor was it? OMG, got to wake up! It wasn't in Tor because it can't be in Tor. Well, technically it could be I guess, I don't really know, but since you can't cache TOR, it would not be. And he wasn't. He's been up all night decoding ICQ files. 3) I'm blown away. For him to have been doing this, he accessed them after we left or let's just say he somehow had them. Wow. Vikram Patel, living on the edge! 4) I'm a little jealous it was him and not me that found this and then comes number 5). And this bouncy neuron path is most intriguing of all. Because I realize one of my thoughts is I am really a bit pissed off that I never got an invite to the LARP to begin with. I happen to be very good at it. LARPing. Or at least I think so. At some point, the shmuck running the show had to solicit some people. And I don't understand why I wasn't invited.

Oh yeah, note to self, number five isn't relevant. I don't have $1,000 or even $300, if one wants to lowball the exchange, to go out and spend LARPing. I don't even know people who have $300 to go out and LARP.

Three Hundred Dollars. That's it. Most people don't-can't-won't pay $300 for a LARP event. Which is why it's so exclusive. It serves all of his needs. So somehow, he has to have tapped into a rich person's resource group.

Okay, now my brain is in full force mode and my fingers are flying the words out to the crowd. "Maybe he's a broker and has rich clients? Maybe he's a playboy who hangs out on his yacht with nothing better to do than set up a very elaborate party with his friends?" Ditto that thinking, but substitute drug dealer. Okay. All possible. But still, "if you're going to be anonymous so you can be some kind of thrill killer, wouldn't it make sense to attract more people than just the group you know, and those people would need to 1) get your dark web address and 2) be willing to ante up some serious cash. So maybe, just maybe, he went through some kind of company or broker who hooks rich people up."

"I mean if I wanted to throw a party for people who will ante up that kind of money, I would have to . . ." my fingers still as I try to grab the thought that is hovering on the tip of my tongue but no one's here to read it. Come on, Sid, do not make bad jokes and lose your focus. Think. Okay, you got it. Fingers resume typing, "I would have to make it either for, you know, a big charity event whereby I could reach out to rich, technically savvy people, who might not like that I am anonymous. But maybe they might or, or I might go get a broker who gets rich people to come and my anonymity is part of the whole gist of the deal and kind of what makes it sexy. A new kind of old-school masquerade event thing. Oh, and sorry, Vik. I should have said that was genius."

"Okay, interrupting the lovefest," Ari pings in on my tour de force, stream of typoed consciousness. "Just in case any of you brainiacs were wondering, 'the world is quiet here' is a quote from *Lemony Snicket*. I didn't want to say anything until I could check, but I knew I knew it. I loves my *Lemony Snicket*. Emoticon pink

100

heart, red heart, pink heart." I don't even need to see Ari to know exactly what accompanies her hearts—eyes batting while smiling pretty.

Go Ari!

"It's the slogan for the VFD." She is right, I forgot all about that. "When we grab you by the ankles, where our mark is to be made, you'll soon be doing noble work, Although you be paid."

And as she types, I so remember the rest of it, "When we drive away in secret,

You'll be a volunteer, So don't scream when we tell you: The world is quiet here."

And as the words Ari is typing stop, and as I finish my own recital of those words, I am not only "quiet here," I am sad. And I am seething. This is evil and it's genius. And it's heartbreaking. "You'll be a volunteer." "So don't scream." It's all laid out. Whoever this is, is perverting my childhood stories. And Lemony Snicket is right. It's the great schism and we are who must stop it from breaking away. And I know where we must go to do it.

SIXTEEN

By lunchtime when we all hit the library, our excitement has turned to overtired crankiness. Well, except for Imani. I presume her grumpiness is a result of not having been online last night and therefore feeling left out. Imani's parents do not allow her to have a computer in her room, so there was no way for us to reach her.

"Look," I lean in and whisper, "I think we should start from the beginning of last night, break it down into bullet points so we can vet it before we share anything."

"I don't know, Sid." Jimmy is sitting so his arms are crossed and he's leaning back, tipping the chair away from the table. He's quiet, but not whispering. Detached and kind of cold, not caring, almost, I think, almost surly. "I think we should just send Vikram's info over to Tsarnowsky and let them sort it." He then kind of juts his chin out as though his mouth is throwing words across at me. "You know, they do get paid for this kind of stuff."

Yes, definitely surly with a nice coating of sarcasm. The table is suddenly very quiet. I stare at Jimmy, trying to understand what is happening. Why he is both mad at us and yet kind of checked out? I see Imani quietly move her hand over to his thigh.

Vikram jumps into what has become, surprisingly, deep dark swirling waters, "I agree with Sid. Even if we do nothing but organize the information, it would be good. We all found different pieces and it would seem foolish to let anything we know get left behind."

"And since I couldn't be there last night," Imani says, theatrically putting on a fake, lower-lip sticking-out pout, all while keeping one hand reassuringly on Flynn's knee, "why don't you all bring me up to speed. I will immerse myself back into our saga by playing the role of stenographer and typing, and then I will feel I am back with the in-crowd."

And so as we all slowly, cautiously, begin our catch-up I am happy to learn Vikram hadn't actually done anything illicit. What he had done was go back into the places we had been able to openly search when we started, but this time, armed with a better sense of what we were looking for, or at least something we could use to lead us to what we were looking for. Which, if I hadn't passed out on my keyboard, would have been my personal POA, plan of action or attack. Anyway, Vik found the first part in one of Tessa's notes, which was simply the word "Wanion," with a big old question mark. He didn't know it either, so he looked it up. Wanion is archaic; originally it meant "for in the time of the waning moon." However, even in its archaic past, it had morphed its way into the ever more potent portent "in the unlucky hour." And sadly, after all that work, wanion apparently became a victim of its own unlucky hour and faded from our language. Until now. So with that one word, he began searching.

And while we debate our intel, Imani makes assorted cuts, copies and pastes, and fresh notations. Ari takes a minute to confirm our assumption that the night Tessa Sargentino died there was actually a waning moon. online almanac says, yes. For that matter, it also, ironically, provides confirmation of the other option of interpretation; it was definitely in an unlucky hour. But that much, we kind of already knew.

And so it goes. Until we have exhausted all our thinking and trimmed it into order.

"Great. This is great." I look up from Imani's screen. "Let's send this over to Tsarnowsky, tell him we'll meet him at Platitude's after school and then, tomorrow at lunch maybe, we'll figure out how to get us all invitations for Saturday night."

And before I am finished talking, I catch Imani looking over to Jimmy. One of those unspoken communication things, which puts me right on edge.

Jimmy's eyes bulge back. Imani stares. Finally, Jimmy caves, drops his chair back down to four legs, "Won't work, Sid."

"Of course it will." I am not sure I understand his point but I try. "Well, Tsarnowsky isn't going to be happy and he may try and stop us, but remember, I am Marchioness Winnie Barrowcliffe-Bantam, and honestly, who cares, he can't control us showing up."

"You're right, Sid. He can't control us showing up. But I can." Jimmy's voice starts to rise. "If I miss practice today, I don't start. Coach is already not happy with me, okay. I skipped Sunday's practice."

A "shhhh" from the table across from us cuts through Jimmy's speech. He glances over to them and their "really man?" looks, makes a placating motion and then turns back to me, and even though his volume drops, his intensity does not. "You called and you didn't ask if I had plans; you told me you needed me and I made a choice. That's on me. But I can't make this choice. The LARP falls on Homecoming. I have a game. I will be the starter. It's not up for discussion. Not even this can make me throw that away." And he pauses, but he's not done. "And, if that's not enough, you and I both know my parents would kill me."

Okay, I am thinking, obviously I had missed the entire Homecoming thing, but there still has to be a solution. Before I can decide my best argument, Jimmy comes back at me.

"And you know what else, I can't not study this week. I'm not you, Sid." Jimmy looks directly at me, gives me a small smile, his anger at me, at himself, gone. "You may be the smartest person I know. If I don't do the work, it's going to show."

"But . . ."

"No, Sid," he shakes his head, holding firm, "no buts here. Did you know Imani nearly flunked her last math exam?"

Obviously I did not. I look over at Imani, and she nods, confirming Jimmy's rant. I am suddenly feeling very small.

"It's okay. Look, we all wanted to do this." Jimmy takes his time and lets Vikram and Ari nod with him. "We all still do. It's just that you can manage all of it better than we can."

Imani quietly elbows Jimmy, while making eye motions to the rest of us. We realize with horror that our intense and on-our-feet discussion has prompted Ms. Nosy-Body Library Lady Stewart to take an interest in us and she is moving rapidly within eavesdropping distance.

Quickly we resettle into chairs and pull them around the table, circling our wagons as it were. I go back to whispering, trying not to cry. "So what am I supposed to do now?"

"You get to take the lead, Sid." Jimmy leans over, grasping my shoulders, forcing me to look at him, "which if we're both honest, is kind of what you've been doing anyway. None of us would have been here if it wasn't for you. Even the cops might not have figured out where she was. So you, you go see our favorite detectives. Bring them up to speed."

And I know he's right about my having taken the lead, but taking the lead when you have a posse is one thing; going it alone is another. So I have to ask. Because, even though I am afraid of the answer, I need to know. My hands start folding a sheet of paper over and over, an old pattern. I focus on them as I try sound blasé and not to whine. "What about the LARP?"

"Imani and I will come as soon as we can get out of my homecoming stuff. I promise. The way I see it, game, dinner with folks, appearance at dance, and we're heading over to you. You'll send us a text where to find you and we'll race as soon as we can."

I flip the piece of paper about my fingers trying to process all of this. Jimmy Flynn, my forever knight, wants me to go without him.

"Um, Ari and I will go with you, Sid." Vikram pipes up. "I know it's not the same for you, but . . ." his voice trails off.

"No. It's not the same." I say out loud agreeing with him, but not for the reason he is assuming. "I thought we'd be the fearsome five. You know, Three Musketeers, Fantastic Four, Fearsome Five." And in my vision of events, you could tell each one of us from the best backlighting angle of sun as we would all have our own individual strut. You know, we'd make our approach and Imani would be our cat walker and Jimmy would, of course, swagger. Ari, you would sashay or maybe flounce and bounce, and Vikram, hmmm, Vik you, you would, stroll, I think. And me, I would stride wide with a glide. Fearsome. We would be so freaking fearsome.

"Well, we may only be three," Ari interrupts my Marvel-esque vision, "but we can still be as fabulous as if we were five. I mean, let's be honest, Sid. I am fabulous enough to count for two and, well, with a little work you . . ."

Jimmy cuts Ari off before she can finish, "A little?"

And we all laugh, because sometimes even I can take a joke. Jimmy looks at the piece of paper I've been playing with and deliberately positions his hands on the table, forming a goalpost. I look up at him, smile wryly. His eyebrow raises up. Is that a dare? I meet his eyebrow and line up my not-since-the-seventh-grade origami football. My fingers flick. I shoot.

Touchdown. Rubin.

¤ ¤ ¤

And so with my epic posse of cheerleading friends standing right beside me, I text our detectives and set an appointment to meet them at Platitude at four o'clock, which should give me enough time to get there, right after I spend an hour at Perk This, helping Imani with her math homework. Color me highly caffeinated.

SEVENTEEN

I zoom in, wave to "our waitress," toss my bag into the booth, then slip right behind it sliding rather deftly into my side. I reach in the front pocket, pull out a folder with three copies of the information, distribute it to the twosome across the table, and proclaim, "Ta Dah!" The whole process couldn't have taken more than thirty seconds.

And before either detective can speak, I start 'splaining, going a mile a minute. "See Wanion means Waning but it can also be unlucky and if you take that and add the hollowed ground bit, you get to Bryant Park, which is where she was found, because nobody really remembers, or cares, but Bryant Park was where they buried the bodies as an overflow potter's field during the yellow fever epidemic, which is exactly where you found her, which of course makes these pieces a perfect invitation to where Tessa met her death." And as I come up for air, I sixth sense something, which, since I have been in archaic word land, I will call collywobbles. But I'm not letting them rise up because I am not finished yet. "And to further prove this connection, we would be willing to bet, although you didn't actually disclose it, she was found bound under or next to one of the carvings of the cattle heads, which used to predict sacrifices to the gods in Ancient Greece." Yeah.

And I stop, look up, expecting an ooh and an ahh for the Bryant Park rationale connecting to the first partial invitation we found, which gives them a solid link for this being the same dude. I expect them to be dazzled by my moment of stupefying genius, demonstrated by perhaps a round of applause. You know, a huge triumphant moment.

Instead, as my collywobbles take root, I catch Detective Tsarnowsky and Detective Macdonald exchanging looks, which I would describe as . . . what's the word I want . . . the look is similar but not exactly like Jimmy's and Imani's. Got it. They are complicit. That's exactly what that look is. Complicit. I take a minute and pick at the corner of the plastic menu, sorting my thoughts.

Thought one: They already know.

Thought two: They told someone.

Thought three: They know because they told someone, someone who isn't us.

And I look up at them, watching them shift uncomfortably, and I know I am right. "I suppose there's no point in explaining *Lemony Snicket* either."

"You know, Sid, I really am sorry." Tsarno looks directly at me. "We didn't really have a choice. When I first asked for your help, I thought, great, you know what something called a LARP is, you'll tell me there was one down in the Village that night, and we would take it from there."

Raspberry blow. Knuckle crack. Lean in. Resume talking.

"Look. Without you guys, I don't know that we could have gotten here. But once we got here, it was too high-tech complicated for us and it was too dangerous for you. It needs more manpower and we, Emma and I, have an obligation to our victim. And you know what else? We have as big, if not bigger, an obligation to you. And to your parents."

And as Detective Tsarnowsky searches my face, looking to see if I am hearing him, I avoid all direct eye contact. I do clench my jaw and let my knee bounce a thousand miles a minute. Fortunately I have my own bench.

Emma takes over the sympathy talk. "Sid." Okay. My jaw clenches tighter, my knee bobs faster. "Sid, it's not something we wanted to do." I want so badly to stick my fingers in my ears and say, *la la la, I can't hear you*, but she is still talking. "It's just something that had to be done."

I know there was more yacking, more asking me to understand, more about what would they say to my parents, and just
more. Then it was over. And I escaped, back up to the High Line,
where I could be alone in a crowd.

¤ ¤ ¤

But I had to come down and share the news with everyone. We
weren't heroes. We weren't going to save the day. We were just a
group of kids and we'd been used.

And as you can imagine, this led to rounds of how much this
sucks. Which led to rounds of grievances. It was time to spin the
wheel of teenage angstxiety and play BitchWhineMoan. And I
don't actually remember how the train of thought led to it exactly,
but I do know it was Ari who looked at all of us and said, "Well,
why don't we just go? I mean, maybe we aren't going as part of,
pause for emphasis to allow her hands to make air quotes, 'the
team,'" but hey, it's a party, and who's to say we aren't on the list?"

And as I explained when we began this journey, for those of you
paying attention, teenagers have underdeveloped frontal lobes.
Teenagers also have FOMO, in spades. And Fear of Missing Out
trumps rational thinking any, and every, day.

All hands into the circle. "Gimme a Hell Yeah! Fear the Five!"

EIGHTEEN

And now let the crazy begin. We have so much to do between this morning, which is Tuesday, just in case you lost track and then Saturday night. And we have very limited hours to work with.

Top priority: wangling invitations. Entering the website is not a big deal. When we left the station, I had the address memorized and then put it in my phone, but honestly how do we buy our invitations? I look around at the posse. "I don't have that kind of money."

"Maybe we all just show up being fabulous," Ari says, "and hope we can get in as just part of the crowd?" I am guessing we are all wearing our rather dubious faces, since when she continues, I sense a tinge of the defensive. "I have to say, guys, it generally works just fine for me."

As Mom would say, rather drolly, "Quelle surprise." But then again, I am not offering up any better ideas.

And we're all standing around, staring at each other, then shifting and looking away, when the bell rings and we grab backpacks and such to head inside. Vik reaches the door and suddenly calls out to us all, "Skip the library, let's meet back here." And with our usual assortment of shrugs, "why not," we head off to class.

¤ ¤ ¤

"It's okay," Vikram waits until we all move around the side of the building. "I will cover the Bitcoins."

Whoa. Watch four mouths drop at once. No one is saying a

113

word. Not even Ari, and she dates him! Finally Imani, she of poise, manners and very political upbringing speaks up. "Vikram, that is very kind and generous of you, but I could not pay such a gift back."

Three heads nod like a set of cheap bobblehead dolls in the back window of an old Chevy.

"No. You don't need to pay it back. My father was an early adopter of Bitcoins. He believes it is the way of the future. So when they came on the market, he made each of his children find work and earn enough to buy one hundred coins."

We all share a collective gasp.

I can't tell you what anyone else here is thinking exactly, but I can tell you I am thinking, and muttering, "And I think my parents are abusing me when I have to clear the table to earn my allowance. Time for a rethink on that one."

Vikram laughs, "No. That's the point. I paid less than a dollar a coin. And when it hit a value of $1,000, my father made us sell half of them to have a college fund. The next forty we are required to hold in case the trading value should ever pierce $2,000. But," and here is where his face lights up with a big smile and he reminds me of the day at the police car, "we were each allowed ten coins for anything we wanted. I think my brothers and sisters have all spent theirs, but I did not have anything I particularly wanted." And again, his smile just beams. "Until today. Today, I want to take my friends to a LARP."

We all go back and forth; can we accept this or can't we accept this? Ari keeps telling him he's been holding out on her. She had no idea he was a rich boy. Imani is unsure. Jimmy thinks it's fair. If he had it, he would do it. I, deep down honestly, am only giving lip service to all of this. I just want to go and if Vikram wants to take us—I shrug internally—that works for me.

With two minutes left before the bell, we decide we will all pick names and put together an outfit; Vikram will buy only three tickets: his, Ari's, and mine. Since Jimmy and Imani can't come until late and by then we should either be able to sneak them in or declare it all a bust, we'll keep in touch by text and then wing it if need be.

As for the Marchioness Winnie Barrowcliffe-Bantam, we all agree, she is most likely now the alter ego of one Detective Emma Macdonald and had best be left behind.

¤ ¤ ¤

Class bell rings, we race out. Jimmy to practice, Imani and I to Perk This for a math tutoring session, and Vikram and Ari to the Public Library to generate names for us all and Bitcoin the three of us in.

The pinging of our phones interrupts. Imani and I both check our texts and laugh. "You first," I say.

"Medician Louisa Goodwin-Goldfinch." Who apparently is from the Southern Steampunk Clan as Imani is suddenly channeling her inner Tara and fanning herself with her napkin. "Papa will be so proud."

"Charmed," I say. And then I stand up, give a little bow, "Air Marshall Percival Coldicott-Stoker, at your service." And for some reason, I feel a need to click my heels, which get caught on the edge of the annoying velvety drape, sending me, coffee in hand, sliding toward the table with computers, which would be very bad. Instead, I jerk back and flip over the chair, landing in a most unhappy backside position.

Hilarity ensues. Thankfully, it's interrupted by my personalized ring tone for one Arianna Wilson. Imani and I both make an instant recovery, lunge for my phone. I win.

"Hey Ari." I put her on speaker in an effort to not pant in her ear.

"Did you get them?"

"Yeah. We did. They're pretty great."

"Vik said you said not to give you a female persona. So we didn't. But that's only because Vik is scared of you and he wouldn't let me. I was dying to help you lace up your bustier. Not too late to change your mind, Sid. We'll be so hot."

Imani is out of control laughing and as much as I know Ari is just messing with me, it's working and I can't stop blushing, but I do try to stop it. "Way cool, thanks." Yeah, so lame. And so not working.

"Mmmmm, hot." Ari is definitely not interested in mercy here. "Nice shade of red I can't see, but I knooooow you've taken to wearing."

Imani is now so far gone, she just sits there and yes, snorts, but I ignore them both. I refuse to talk into the phone because I know if I answer this will never end. But even Ari can get bored torturing me and finally, in what I like to see as a great humanitarian gesture, moves on.

"I'm guessing you already know Percival was one of King Arthur's Knights. Vik and I thought it made perfect sense for you, Ms. Holy Grail Hunter. Anyway, let me speak with Imani for a minute." But before I can give Imani the phone, I hear, "Oh, and Sid."

"Yeah."

"I want it on the record, it was very classy of me not to ask you why you were panting so hard when you answered."

So much for her great humanitarian gesture. Ari is back to screeching with laughter; I feel my face exploding yet again into what must now be a red so deep it is borderline purple. Imani takes the phone I am holding out, laughing hysterically herself, because it isn't like she couldn't hear Ari. She is, after all, standing right here.

Imani slowly turns away, cupping the phone with her right hand, still wiping her eyes with her left. And Ari must be off the speaker and even whispering because, unlike before, all I am hearing is Imani's side of the call. "Yeah." Pause. "Yeah." Pause. "Great." She hangs up, hands me back my phone, takes a seat, and looks at me like the cat that ate the canary. And she knows I know and, wait for it, yes, she picks up her hand as though it's a paw and gives it an imaginary lick.

Apparently I am going to have to ask. "Well?"

"So glad you asked." White teeth fake smile alert. "Tomorrow,

116

after I ace my math test, thank you, we are all going shopping, including you. We need outfits, including you. And we need them to work. So we are going to hit every single thrift store in the city until they're perfect! And in this case, perfect is something only you can help us determine!" Imani knows just how evil she is being as she looks directly at me, letting her words register.

And she knows they have scored as she throws back her head and laughs maniacally.

I hate to shop.

¤ ¤ ¤

Seventeen. Seventeen freaking thrift shops and two days later we have what Imani and Ari deem the "starting pieces" for our outfits. We have two used tux jackets—one with tails and one pinstriped, three pairs of tux pants, one of them white, and one brown bomber jacket, three shirts that will give us standing collars and one bow tie plus two wide ties. We have one white restaurant apron with black skirt and super cool black belt and one bustier with garter belt, a white see-through slip thing, and a scarf in pale blues and magentas. Care to guess who belongs to what?

In addition, we find eight belts for three dollars, one pair of stilettoes, one pair of spats, one pair of black tall boots with lots of buckles and one pair of mint-condition, old-school spectators, which are a perfect fit for me. Mini-high! Sadly, short lived.

As apparently this is only the beginning. We need monocles and pocket watches, although we do find two we can afford in one of our thrift shop stops, along with ascots and, of course, top hats. And the problem with top hats is we need to find real ones so we don't look like we bought our costume at the local thrift shop, which of course, is exactly what we have done. ARGH!

On the bright side, we needed two distinct fascinators and we actually find them in our travels. I put that under the category "there is a God."

On the downside, we find only one pair of goggles.

Little white lie time. Call parents, tell them we are studying together, which is only half a lie, thus keeping us under the previously declared little white demarcation line, stuff pizza down our throats on the run, and keep moving. Best part about New York City, something is always open for business.

¤ ¤ ¤

Carbs do their trick and the adventure continues as we race from thrift to pawn and manage to shockingly find two more pairs of goggles, the third men's pocket watch, and two women's pendant watches. We also find an old-style leather aviator hat, which saves us at least one yet-to-be-found top hat and a cool copper clock/weathervane thing-y, which Imani shrieks will be "perfect for something!"

As we, or honestly Imani and Ari, are bargaining at the pawn-shop, I am flipping through a box at the register filled with postcards, stickers, and other small items. One reads, "To thrive in life you need three bones. A wishbone. A backbone. And a funny bone. Reba McIntire." I like it. The question is do I like it enough for Mr. Clifton's table? I don't know.

Imani leans over my arm, reads the sticker, makes my decision, and turns to the rather swarthy counter guy. "Okay, sir, throw this in and we're done." She then turns back to me, "We don't have time to debate if this is it. Let's take it. You can argue it to death later. Move!"

Needless to say, I am exhausted.

¤ ¤ ¤

Next day, Vikram joins us as we duck into a hardware store where I think we buy about 500 gears, gauges, and other such wires and chains. Then it's into a fabric store where I think we must buy at least another 500 yards of black lace, a thousand sewing pins with round heads, and jewel bits and bobs and I don't know what all else and at least a zillion yards of ribbon.

And while I understand some of the theory here, I tremble at being called upon to help it come together.

Mercifully, however, we then split up. Vikram and I are ordered to find a discount store and given instructions to buy assorted water guns, black paint, metallic paints and other funky items to insure our weapons and our cell phones are ready, tricked out, and cool. This, my friends, is so not a problem.

¤ ¤ ¤

Our clock is now ticking really scary fast. Imani does manage an A minus on the math exam, so that buys us a few days before we need to panic about numbers again. And more good news: Imani has two cousins who work as seamstresses for the Met Opera costume shop and if we can come by tomorrow night about seven-thirty, they will help us with our costumes for the, um, school play.

How many white lies make a big huge outright lie? Just curious. I'm thinking if we manage to pull this off without being killed by either Tsarno or our parents, we should ask Mr. Clifton to add that question to his course curriculum.

¤ ¤ ¤

Vik and I spend the next afternoon building our weapons and our cell phone casings, which are really critical. They need to be cool, but with the cell phones we have to be careful not to cover up any parts that might complicate basic functions. And of course these covers also have to be able to come on and off as none of us can exactly walk around school with our "new case" showing.

I now know that the only person lamer than me with art-meets-shop skills, or lack thereof, is Vikram Patel.

Wow.

And just when I think it really can't get more complicated than it is, I get home from this frustrating but surprisingly more than acceptable-in-the-end endeavor and run smack into mom who heard my keys in the door. "Hi, Mom." I go for cheerful as I swing down my backpack and give her a kiss on her cheek.

"Bon soir, cherie." Mom steps back and studies me. "Are you feeling okay, Sidonie? I am worried about you. You've been coming home late the last few nights. I am not so old that I do not know everything did not turn out as you had wished, no?

Oh no, start the blush combined with the twist and squirm. "No, Mom, it's all good. It wasn't fun but it's okay. Honest. I was just caught up with tutoring Imani the last few days is all." I want to plead with her to go away, but I know that won't work. It will only reinforce her thinking. Got it. "Ma Mere," I smile, "No avoir le cafard pour moi. Je promets." Add exaggerated, cheesy grin.

Quick sidetrack for a brief backstory moment: *avoir le cafard* is a French expression for having the blues, but its literal translation is to have the cockroach. It has made me laugh delightedly forever and is always a joke between mom and me.

And it still works. Mom smiles, shakes her head, pushes at my hair, which I tolerate well for the bigger cause, rubs the back of her hand down my cheek. I can breathe. All will be fine.

I escape to my bedroom. Rapidly. Drop my bag on the chair and my butt on the bed. And just when I am thinking, "whew," it is now safe to relax, there's a knock on my door, followed by a query. "Sidonie?"

Instant spine alignment. "Oui, Mama?"

Mom sticks her head in the door, also managing to glance around a bit. Not sure what she thinks she might see, but everything is as it should be, at least until she speaks. "I just wanted to remind you we are meeting the Flynns' for dinner after the football game to celebrate. I understand Imani and her parents are coming as well."

To quote Mama, "Merde."

NINETEEN

"Look." Jimmy catches sight of Janelle, the mouth of the south by way of the Bronx, coming down the hall toward us. As it's pouring for all it's worth outside this morning, we are trapped inside the chaos, huddling in the hallway with nowhere to hide. "We can make this work. But we can't talk here. Everybody gets game day jitters. I would know. But we are going to be fine. Library at lunch." With that, he stands, yells out, "Hey, Trey, wait up man!" winks at us, flashes a big grin with a pointer-finger gun pop to Janelle and takes off down the hallway, catching up to the waiting Trey.

"Um. James Flynn?" Imani yells after him, "Did you forget something?"

Jimmy turns back, his books hit Trey's stomach as he zooms back down the hallway, coming in on his knees and looking up with a big smile. "Ah, forgive me, my lady; I don't know what I was thinking." With that, he pops up, bows, kisses her hand and takes off, bowing his way back down the hall, laughing hysterically.

Giddy are we. Apparently.

But we manage to make it to lunch and the rain has stopped, so we relocate ourselves outside because it seems Ms. Stewart has gotten way too nosy for our own comfort.

"I timelined everything." Jimmy picks up where we left off this morning. "It's going to be close, but I think we've got this. We spend tonight at Imani's cousins doing final fittings and everything else. Tomorrow's game is in the afternoon. The dance is at night, but it starts at eight, the same time you guys have to be at the LARP to quote, play your part." Jimmy pauses, his hand and eye motions running a check down as though he is now in the pocket, quarterbacking his team.

"This means I can tell my folks we have to be done with dinner early as Imani and I need to dress for the event, because," he pauses for an uncharacteristic bout of eye and head bob of embarrassment, "I will be named Homecoming King and we want to get there on time and look great."

"Which gets you," Jimmy points to me, "on your way I would think by seven o'clock. And that should be enough time for you to change and get there before eight, yes?"

"And we," Vikram motions to Ari and himself, "we can go early and hold a place if there's a line or something. We would easily be in the park to meet you by seven. We can even bring your costume with us, Sid."

"And when you think about it," Jimmy resumes his train of thought, "it honestly works out perfect. Imani and I will leave right after my 'dance as king' and head to you. None of us have to explain anything because everyone's parents think we are at the dance. Which they all know won't end early."

I would like to let myself think of this plan as a God shot, but that would be duplicitous, even by my standards.

But Jimmy sticks out his hand, waits for just a second, and we stack ours right on up. "Okay everyone, tonight we dress, for tomorrow we success."

OMG! He has so lost it!

And he's not done. We're still gathered around in our huddle and Jimmy looks at me, smiles, and says, "Let me get a Fearsome Five!"

Hands in, we give him just that!

TWENTY

So I am now racing across Ninth Avenue on my way to Forty-second so I can cut down to our meeting place at Bryant Park. And with each step, the Five Napkin's hamburger threatens to not keep its downward esophageal track. Really Flynn? You had to pick burgers, shakes and fries? Ugh. I know. I know it's the best burger. But really, we needed burgers for Homecoming dinner?

In fairness, you did sacrifice the best steak house in the city for this much speedier option. And I did not have to have the cheese and the bacon and the onion rings with the shake. I also did not have to choke it all down as there was no way I was getting out of there ahead of anybody else. So much of this threatening upchuck is sadly of my own doing.

TMI. I know. I will now attempt to get my mind off my stomach. I will bring you up to speed.

Last night at Imani's cousin's house: an absolute zootacular. But it did come with great food. As our cost for the alterations, we were required to bring Korean barbecue from their favorite neighborhood dive, and it was truly scrumptious.

Imani's cousins are Lita and Ayisha and when they saw how much stuff we had, they called two of their gay-boy friends, Marcus and Tyrell, to come over and help. And they looked at us, looked at our collection, proclaimed us "geniuses," and promised we would be "fabulous." And by the time they were finished, we were definitely that.

The genius part is they made Flynn's outfit using the tux and the top hat, and Imani's outfit using the black skirt with a magnificent scarf they had and tons of lace. This way they could go straight from the dance to the LARP without needing to change.

Okay. Pause for a second. I'm at Forty-second. Breathe. Wait for the light. Head down the Avenue.

Anyway, I can't describe all of us in detail because I needed to head out before the rest. Given my parents latest concerns, I thought staying out too late would be stupid. And Imani, who always has a stricter curfew than the rest of us, didn't have to leave with me, as her parents were fine with her visiting her cousins. Just a little bitter irony here.

So, as I now race up to the park, thinking "bitter, party of one," while huffing loudly and looking around, I see Vikram wave and nudge Ari, and I lose whatever breath I have been working to recover.

Wow. They both look ridiculously, outrageously, fine.

Vikram sees me look and spins, showing off what, at first glance, is a very simple outfit—basically a black shirt with standing collar, black tie, black pants, and black long coat. With that, he has a black top hat and black goggle glasses. Nothing has any adornment on it. But what it does have is an entire overlay of mechanical nonsense beginning on his right shoulder and ending fitted on his right-hand fingers, which have a partial glove thing to hold this contraption in place. It has gauges and gears and a big, copper metal hose thing and it's freaking awesome.

"Marcus and Tyrell built it for me this morning." Vikram is grinning ear to ear. "Isn't it amazing?" He pulls back his coat and shows me the holster on his leg, made with belts and whatever. "It holds the gun in here." Then he shows me an inside coat pocket; "they even made a place for the phone. They did something similar for Jimmy, but his entire outfit is in black and white. It's really awesome. And . . ."

Before Vikram can continue, a riding crop hits the ground between all of us. "Ahem." Ari interrupts and struts herself directly in between Vikram and me, directly into my eyeline and poses, tipping back her bowler style hat, slowly turning toward her right.

"Wowzerhole."

One entire side of her face is done in gears, which travel down her neck, disappearing into her chest, which is, of course, loosely concealed by a white shirt with lace overlay, all lifted up by a bustier. To complete the look, she has on a striped short skirt, black hose with a side lace cutout pattern thing going on, and stilettoes. And I mean stilettoes. They are black and they are super tall and the backside heel is all done in gears, which match her face.

Let's practice KISS and keep it simple. Arianna Wilson is hot. Scorching hot.

She looks at me staring at her, and obviously I am delivering exactly what she wants to see because she throws her head back, vamps, and laughs. Then Ari snaps and turns to Vik, grabs a bag, and thrusts it at me. "Change, NOW."

I look around for a bathroom and can't spot one, so I whisper, "Where?"

"Here. We'll use that bush, Vik will turn around and keep an eye on one side, and I will distract from the other."

Here? In the open? Where people walk by? Is she insane?

Ari stares at me, her patience rapidly waning. I walk over to the tree. If I were theatrical, I would walk resignedly over to the tree, dragging my feet and stumbling every two inches. But I admit, I accepted my current lot in life rather meekly and awkwardly.

Satisfied, both Ari and Vik turn around and form a rather none-too-solid wall around me.

"Okay, so while you were out stuffing your face, Vik and I got down to the park to do some super sleuthing for us."

Scan quickly, coast looks reasonably clear. Well, let me clarify that: coast is filled with people in the park, but none of them seem interested in me. Perhaps a couple of them seem to be very interested in Ari, which makes me realize I am invisible as long as I stay behind her. Dropping my pants while keeping my shirt on while pulling on the new ones and, voila, dressed. This Ari-as-distract-ress could prove very useful for future reference. Done. Button fly. Sweet detail. These really are pretty cool, two pairs cut down to make one with one leg white and one leg black.

125

"So anyway, we met this guy. His costume sucks by the way. He says there will be role player characters coming by who will tell the first group of us what we're supposed to be doing. He says he was at the last one and it was insane. That the role players get scripts and parts to kick things off and there was a ton of booze and a bunch of super-rich tech guys and stuff. But he wouldn't give us his name, and he wouldn't say where the last one was so we could confirm he definitely meant the Tessa one, but he did finally say he thinks the dude throwing the LARP is some Asian guy."

Vik interrupts here and clarifies, "Satoshi Nakamoto."

"Really?" It comes out more snort than questions as I check around again, slip my arms out of my sleeves, while still leaving T-shirt on and then slip the white button up shirt on under the cover my T-shirt provides. I leave the arms with the oversized lacey cuffs open and dangling while I button the front. "As in the guy who invented the whole Bitcoin system?" Shirt buttoned, I glance around once more as I now discard my T-shirt and work on closing the sleeves. I spot something familiar across the way, but shake it off and keep going until I am fully covered with the basics. "By the way, thanks, you can turn back around."

Vik turns back and continues the story, "This is the guy's logic. He thinks that is why it takes Bitcoins to get in."

Next item in the bag is the vest. Black and white stripes with oversized collar. It's double breasted. Wonder if it used to be a blazer. And, yes, it has an interior cell phone pocket. "Great." I pause to fit my cell phone in said pocket and then lean back down to fish more items from the bag.

"Big no-help there. Since Satoshi Nakamoto is a pseudonym, and no one knows who he really is, it won't matter if dude's right or not, we still wouldn't know who to look for." Pull pre-square-knotted black tie, thank you boys, over my head. Wow. This is one big holster, fitting the belt part around my waist and the other tie around my leg. Next. Lacey band stretchy things? Hmmm. Got it. "But for the record, he's wrong." Armbands for over the shirt sleeves. "I mean not that I actually know. And he obviously could afford to rent the library out and all that." Black and copper goggles. "I just find it hard to believe Satoshi Nakamoto, who nobody knows, is hanging out at our local Public Library throwing a LARP, even an ultra-exclusive one." A white top hat! Digging that. And finally, on the very bottom, my personal piece de resistance, my tres, tres cool shoes, my very own black and white spectators.

And when I slip them on, I realize I am the steampunk version of Eliot Ness, G-man. So freaking amazing.

"Wow." Ari gives me a wolf-whistle. Adjusts my hat. And my tie. But I draw the line at her "adjusting" my gun, which she is now holding, as it is not fitting into my holster. I just take it from her and go to tuck it away all by myself, which gets me a set of pursed lips and an air kiss, but she does continue. "So according to this guy, these other guys will come through and give us various assignments. And we might not be together, because it's all about assigning roles for the script we are playing."

As the three of us exchange looks, I also give up on holstering my weapon. I had made it a kind of grappling gun by using a toy batman hook thing, and let's just acknowledge that all attempts to holster the bat wings are pointless. Besides, the clock continues to tick and we have maybe ten minutes left to think of something brilliant.

"Maybe we should stop and think about this." Oh no, Vikram, now is not the time to make me not like you again. "I mean, what if they do split us up?" Vikram's voice betrays his nervousness. "We cannot be calling each other every five seconds. And there is a killer in there somewhere."

Okay. That's not going to be the something brilliant we need. Really, Vikram, now is not the time for cold feet. Come on, think, Sid, think. Got it.

I scan the trees toward where I saw that quasi-familiar movement earlier. "Hey, Jean," I suddenly scream out.

Vik looks at me confused. "Your brother?"

"Yeah. The stupid slagamorph's been following me for days. Thinks I don't actually know. Well now, now my friends, we are going to make him a useful stupid slagamorph."

127

TWENTY-ONE

The bushes part and Jean stumbles as he approaches, his too-big-for-his-own-feet body tripping over his gait, which seems to be caught in a tug of war between the dueling energy twins: eagerness and wariness. I roll my eyes while I pick up the bag with my clothes. I realize I have not made any arrangements for them and will now have to try and hide them in a bush or something, and then hope they don't disappear.

And as I watch Jean literally trip his way over, I realize I am watching my solution approach. Thus, I realize I can afford to be charitable about his slip and not say something like, "have a nice trip there?" as, if he does nothing else, he will be good for schlepping.

"Here." We have no time to waste. I shove the bag at him. "Try and keep up with us." I look at Ari and Vikram and we start hustling. "We have seven minutes to get there."

"We have a job for you." Jean runs alongside me, intent on every word. "You know Marauder's Map?" I pause for just a second. "And not the Hogwart's magical one, the app by Aran Khanna?" I hear the grunt. "Okay, it's still available, but only on an open source website. You need to get it and build it now." I stop, waiting for his confirmation. It is critical that he understand this part.

Jean looks directly at me, nods, and then we race on. Seconds are now counting here. "While you are doing that," I raise my voice to ensure Vik and Ari can hear, "we are all going up to Facebook Messenger and getting on the same thread." I see the thumbs up from Vikram.

129

I continue with his mandate. "You are going to use that app to track our latitude and longitude, which will show you exactly where we are. And you are going to find Detective Tsarnowsky and share it all with him."

And I watch for a moment as he smiles the biggest smile while his fingers race across his phone. Satisfied, I turn and look at the rest of us, "Facebook Messenger, NOW."

¤ ¤ ¤

And as I say, " NOW," we arrive at the where of it all. We are at the bottom of the front steps of the New York Public Library. Where, as Lemony Snicket might tell us, the readers go because readers are good people. And judging from the crowd, so are LARPers.

And, as the clue said, the world is quiet here. Only not exactly right this second. There are top hats and aviator hats, fascinators and ascots, parasols and bustiers, weapons and props all creating a party atmosphere as everyone chats and flits and mills and otherwise contributes to a low-level, constant buzz. I have landed at the steps of cosplay heaven. Wow.

GONG! The buzz falls, silenced by the clang of a gong reverberating loudly, whipping the crowd around so fast it allows an illusion that we are choreographed to look up as one. When we do, we see a theatrical smoke display unleashed at the top of the entrance in front of the Roman-style columns. From behind the columns and the smoke, six fully masked, goggled, and steampunked behemoths emerge.

I am trying to take it all in, while simultaneously fiddling with my phone, my suddenly too-fat fingers struggling to turn my location setting back on in the Facebook app. I can see Vikram is stunned, frozen, his mouth agape, watching the spectacle. I hope he has already put a message on the thread. I also hope he helped Ari, as I am not positive she was following it all. I glimpse what must be the main guy stepping forward, standing with his hands behind his back, waiting, checking all of us out. As he gets our full attention, he brings his hands forward, displaying an oversized scroll for us to see and then, deliberately, he unfurls it.

I get the location setting reset and stash my phone just as the guy begins to read.

If you have not come
to play your part,
Leave this stage
to those with heart.

For only those
Who will die for their art
Shall find comfort here

Big deliberate pause.

At our LARP

The crowd cheers!

As big behemoth dude speaks, I scan the gathering crowd and realize there must be well over the allotted hundred people already inching forward. Before dude can finish his recitation, I spit out the order "Move now" to Ari and Vikram and start to race up the steps. I leap directly past Patience and Fortitude, giving them not a moment's thought, jostling for position, trying to gain enough real estate to be picked.

And as my hand is touched by LARPer number two from the left, I turn back to see if I can spot Ari or Vik even as the wave of players pushes me farther in. I don't see them, but I do see a big ill-fitted guy struggling, rapidly losing ground. One step up and two pushed back. Gadzooks! It's Tsarno the Barno. I'd know that physique anywhere. He really should have asked us for help with his outfit. Wow. I know he's not going to make it. No salmon upstream swimming for him. I lift my goggles in an effort to reach out and make eye contact. I can't see his face, so I can only hope he is seeing mine as I mouth, "Find Jean," even as the surging crowd swallows me up.

¤ ¤ ¤

In the majestic marble entry of Astor Hall we are gathered, but divided into what are apparently our separate groups. And there seem to be six of those, one for each of the—I don't know what exactly—oversized leader people? I spot Ari in a group standing in the stairwell, but Vikram is not with her. It is nervously quiet inside. The main door is still open as we hear the head leader guy turn the rest away.

> *For those of You*
> *Not in this part,*
> *Do not leave, for*
> *At nine it will start*

He's got a really beautiful voice. I wonder if it's just his regular voice, or if he's trained or something. Reminds me of Captain Jean-Luc Picard. I keep searching through the chosen hundred, searching for Vikram, yes, but also looking for what, or who, I don't know, when I suddenly realize that straight across from me, I am staring directly at the Marchioness Winnie Barrowcliffe-Bantam. And you know, the detective is not looking all that happy to see me. But I have to say, she is rocking that corset and those thigh-high boots. And her eyes are smoking hot. I wonder if she did them herself. Ooh La La. La La.

I flash her my best gentlemanly grin, accompanied by a very slight tip of my hat. Her only response is a continuation of the not-too-happy-look, this time accompanied by a slight nudge to the person next to her. Although she is subtle, I see it and take note. Must be another one of "their" team. I wonder if she has figured out Tsarno didn't make it in.

But before I can wonder any more, Captain Jean-Luc dude returns, interrupting our moment. The doors close behind him.

132

And he strolls casually and yet deliberately into the center, positioning himself so he is lit perfectly by the light rays streaming through the three enormous windows. I finally catch sight of Vikram over with the far left group. So at least we all made it inside.

"My name is Inquisitor," he pauses for effect, his voice deeply, assuredly filling the room. "Cyrus," Porteus," pause, "Stamford," pause, "Robur."

As in Robur the Conqueror? So much for my thinking Captain Picard.

And as our beautifully backlit, insanely sonorous Inquisitor Robur continues his address to the room, slowly turning, from group to group, person to person, Conqueror makes perfect sense. Because if I wanted to look away, I don't think I could. He is totally compelling. At least six-foot-six and filled with, I don't know, charisma maybe? Maybe power?

"You may have noticed you each have been assigned a group and an Officer of My Court. My officers were once very much like you, a rag tag teeming populace, brought before me seeking favors. They were not successful. For their crimes, each of them was given an *elinguation.*" He stretches out the word, letting all four syllables have their moment, pausing, waiting, letting us all know how critical this is. "A cutting out of their tongue."

Oh no. There is definitely no Captain Jean-Luc Picard here. Wow. I may have to do penance for that one when this is all over.

And as Inquisitor Robur continues, I try hard to think who, or what, he reminds me of. There's a bit of a cyborg about him, but not really. Maybe it's supposed to be a Roman Emperor meets the Victorian Era, but no, that doesn't really fit either. And you know, as I furtively glance about, I may have boasted about having been to several LARPS before, mostly dystopian, but I can honestly say, nothing was even remotely like this.

I take a moment to tuck back, hiding in my so-called group of, I think, twelve, to push another "send" from my messenger, just in case. I'm thinking there may not be another opportunity for a while.

133

TWENTY-TWO

We are on the move. I was right; there are a dozen of us in my group. It's interesting. Assuming we are the one hundred of us "as advertised," the groups are not divided equally. Three groups, including mine, make their way into Room 117, home of the Lionel Pincus and Princess Firyal Map Division.

As mythology has been told, our fearless group leader has "no tongue" so we are motioned toward the back where we form a semicircle, keeping our backs turned away from the rest of the room. From a box on the table, we are handed a page of notes to work with. The first line explains we will be servers. It continues to explain it is our job to raise $400 per person from the crowd for a total of $4,800. Fifty percent of the money will be ours to keep for our night's "work"; the other fifty percent will be distributed to associates whose work does not allow the same level of entrepreneurship.

The only good news here is everyone else in my group seems as unsure as I feel. I know I didn't come here to work to pay for this, especially when I or, more honestly, Vikram, has already given.

But although we all shift uncomfortably, no one says anything. Confusion? Fear? Apprehension? Aw heck, let's just go with a bit of all three.

However, before I can think of a best course of action, props, mostly serving trays and tip jars, but also a bunch of coins, apparently for making change, is distributed. And thus the money is LARP money and we are not here to hustle. Okay. I am at least feeling better for this clarification. I am not sure I am feeling better about anything else yet.

I have to say, the coins are actually pretty cool. They are some kind of metallic coating over what may have been checker pieces or something, but they are actually embossed with steampunk designs. According to our notes, the watch piece is a one, the propeller is a five, the wings are a twenty, and the nautilus is a hundred. We have five watch pieces and two propellers. As I turn them over in my hands, I'm hoping I can keep a full set at the end of the night.

But for now, I calmly flip my propeller and, jinkies, manage to miss it. Darn! As I grab it from the floor, I glance over toward Vikram.

I quickly count sixteen in his group and watch as they are now getting handed several props. First comes a scarlet red sash and then it looks like they are getting a bunch of ribbons with medals on them, gold braids and some kind of . . . telescopes—the kind you see in pirate movies when the lookout guy on the ship looks over the bow and says, "land ho."

Vikram catches me looking, slips his sash on, and makes a big puff of a chest move so I can see the medals. He takes his telescope, with its brass and leather trim, expands it open and then slips it back.

In return, I stick out my tongue at him and flash my serving tray. Big whoop.

Vikram turns back around, ending our moment, as the guy next to him gives him an elbow. He is handed what looks like a rolled-up flag, maybe?

I continue my room surveillance, now under pretense of working on my tray balance.

The third group is really surprising to me. I actually know a few of them. Not in the personal sense, but rather from the streets. They're a bunch of buskers, street performers, and at least a couple of them are musicians, and the only reason I know them is I recognize the outfits. They have some very cool outfits, which I have admired in passing. And it's kind of weird to see them here, because I can't imagine buskers anteing up a bunch of hard-earned Bitcoins for this, but then again, what do I know?

I do know that neither the group with Ari, nor the group with Emma Macdonald, is in this room. But I'm not really worried about that. Yet. I am thinking that since we are taking up a lot of the space, they're probably next door also being outfitted for this evening's festivities. And if Ari were sent off alone, Jean should know. So by my theorizing, in this room we are somehow accounting for serving, protecting maybe, and entertaining. Can't wait to see what else we are here to do.

¤ ¤ ¤

The wait is not long. We are led back into Astor Hall and positioned by groups. Since we have been gone, tables and other event venue items have been brought in and placed throughout. My group is stationed near the bar area, where we are lined up, trays at our side, service ready.

Vik is climbing the stairs with his group and as they near the top, they are spread out in pairs, one with spyglass at the ready and one who appears to be that one's second. The center opening is left empty. I see Ari and Emma Macdonald pass by. They are with seven other women and they are apparently, I am guessing, ladies of the night. They are positioned to form a gauntlet as the guests come through the door. Okay, so not fair. Ari and Emma seem to have made themselves into a terrible twosome as they strike poses, or "make shapes" as the fashion industry likes to say. And fine shapes they are. Oh yes, I am definitely staring. But wait, vision interruptus, there's a bunch of movement as another ten or so, who seem to be beggars, join their party. And before they finally clear to the left, and I get to return to my unimpeded view, I realize one of them also looks vaguely familiar, but I'm not sure.

But clear they do and look I do, and when Ari spots me she winks and blows a huge kiss. Then she throws back her head and laughs and I know it's because she knows I am mortified. Mostly at being caught staring.

Fortunately, distraction is at hand as more props come flying in with another group being hustled into the room. They are carrying velvet ropes and red carpets to place and have epaulets added to their wardrobes. I think it is fairly safe to assume they are some type of greeter group. The ropes get strung out so the pauper people are on the outside of the red carpet aisle.

And when we have all taken our places, our favorite Inquisitor does one more walk about the room and then signals to someone.

Suddenly we hear trumpets outside and all the lights inside are turned off. The front doors open and the head honchos step outside. Upon their exit, the musicians enter, while the gathering outside, judging from the bits we can hear inside, is organized. They are led in by lantern light, through the roped-in red carpet and take up space in the lobby. When everyone is in, the Inquisitor climbs the steps, followed by his court. They light their way, and train our eyes, with the lanterns they are carrying. As they reach the second floor, they spread out across the balcony, taking over the empty center space.

Inquisitor Robur is handed some kind of rod thing, which he then bangs on the floor three times.

The court drops their masks and parts of their clothing and, all at once, I get it. Cyrus was the engineer who was a former Union soldier and his "Court" is made up of the freaking Cannibals. Who are now reasonably half-naked in their punk.

Three more bangs on the floor.

All the lanterns go black and from somewhere a different switch is turned on and if I thought I had just been mind-blown, I was wrong. I am awestruck. As in struck with awe. As in flabbergasted. As in Holy Shit.

It *is* Jules Verne's Nautilus. Jules. Verne's. Freaking. Nautilus. And we are standing here, ready to board.

It's the most insanely brilliant, beautiful thing I've ever seen. Using lights and drapes and backdrops and whatever sleight of eye, like the velvet rope entrance, it's all been created. For us. For a LARP.

And before anybody recovers their, what's that word? French

origin. Means composure, but more than that. Means almost their "vertical-ness." Got it, their aplomb, a voice speaks. "Welcome, my friends."

I start looking around, but I can't see where it's coming from. "Before you come aboard, remember one thing . . ."

I know it's projecting from some speakers, but I can't get a fix on who is speaking or where he is. I am hoping either Ari or Vik are getting a better view. I manage to catch Ari's eye, but she just shrugs. And since she can see the entire balcony, I'm thinking whoever is speaking is not visible to any of us.

"On the surface, they can still exercise their iniquitous laws, fight, devour each other, and indulge in all their earthly horrors. But thirty feet below the surface, their power ceases, their influence fades, and their dominion vanishes . . . There I recognize no master!"

And as the voice finishes, we hear the rod rap the floor again. Vikram and some other guy on the other side of the balcony step forward and unfurl flags. As the motto *Mobilis in mobili* is revealed, the crowd below starts cheering. It is absolutely perfect theater.

And yes, the quote is Captain Nemo all right. I am thinking only one thing. This is freaking insane. It may not be exactly what Jules Verne had in mind at the time. But it is still so clearly Jules Verne and it is ridiculous.

And as the cheering pauses, the voice continues: "So let me tell you that you will not regret the time spent on board my vessel. You are going to travel through a wonderland. Astonishment and stupefaction will probably be your normal state of mind. You will not easily become blasé about the sights continually offered to your eyes. I am going to embark on a new underwater tour of the world—who knows, perhaps the last?—and revisit everything I have studied on my many travels, and you will be my study companion."

And before I can do anything other than register the words, the musicians and buskers flood into the room from where they were hidden behind the lobby. And after a few minutes of fire-eating and body-tossing, during which time the rope lines are pushed to the doors and such, they begin to lead the way up the stairs, assisted by the greeter group, including the new besties, the scarlet harlot twins.

And as I am pondering how all this coordination works, I am hit by a flying ice cube and realize everyone is filling their trays and getting to work, except apparently me. The un-hired help. And in instant answer to my own ponder, this is apparently how all this coordination works. I hand the bartender my weapon to place underneath the bar. Oh my. I watch the tray be filled with a dozen glasses and a small sign, "All Drinks, One Propeller." If only The Flynn were here to see this. And as I hoist my tray, I breathe deep and smile, recognizing this is the most awesome, coolest thing I have ever seen.

TWENTY-THREE

It is, however, instantly less cool as I climb two floors worth of steps while balancing a tray of drinks, and the first flight up to the balcony, for the record, is really a double flight to begin with. So it is really three flights and I am on the edge of letting my joy turn, when I reach the landing and arrive at the Rose Reading Room. And as my drag queen friend, Mint Julep, loves to exclaim, "Shut the Front Door!"

And since Jimmy is not here to say, "Treppenwitz," I will use my gaping mouth moment to make sure you, my friends, can share in my astonishment. The Rose Reading Room is more formally known as The Deborah, Jonathan F. P., Samuel Priest, and Adam R. Rose Main Reading Room. It is 78 feet wide by 297 freaking feet long. Or your basic two city blocks of one gigantic room! The ceilings are fifty-two feet high and they're decorated with paintings of clouds and sky.

And in case that isn't spiritually overwhelming enough, the walls of the room are lined with old-fashioned bookshelves, filled with real, touchable, smell-able books, and the center of the room is a red carpet aisle with long oak tables forming row after row, all lit by bronze lamps. And whoever set this night in motion has taken the room's rich bones and used lighting and props along the north-south length to give the illusion that the walls are slimming in and we are coming aboard a submarine. Pow. Zap. Wow! Welcome to the Grand Salon of the Nautilus.

And now, as my mouth is finally closing, thank you for sharing that, my friends, I am able to see this very magnificent room almost as though it was meant to be. Steampunk is honestly the very essence of what the room demands.

¤ ¤ ¤

And before I can even decide, north end or south, although the band at the far end of the north is rhythmically pulling me that way, my tray is rapidly being drained of its drinks, and ironically I am finding myself feeling pretty good about my earning potential here. That's when I hear, "You know, Sid, you are one royal pain-in-the-ass."

"The name is Air Marshall Percival Coldicott-Stoker." I reply in the spirit of both good roleplaying and warning all while I am counting change for a guest's twenty-dollar wing coin. Although I am thinking that saying dollar is probably a case of poor redundancy or maybe just inaccuracy. I think I would say twenty wing coin, because it wouldn't be dollars, would it? I mean, it could be Euros or pounds or zekadogs, whatever they might be!

Oh Sid. Not now. Now is so not the time for a digression. Focus. Hand the man three propellers at five apiece. Done. Turn attention back to Tsarno. "And you are surprised, Sir? Really?" The part I don't say out loud is, "because that wouldn't make you a very good detective, now would it?" I do say, "Who exactly helped you with your choice of outfit? You do know you are supposed to inhabit it?"

Tsarno grunts. "Just stay out of the way. If it wouldn't blow the entire night, I would have you and your friends cuffed and perp-walked out of here. This isn't television and bad guys don't know they're not supposed to ever hit anyone with their bullets. Clear?"

I nod my understanding of that, because let's be honest, even to get Emma Macdonald's attention, I have not fantasized about being shot at. Not really my thing.

"And if I think you aren't hearing me, I will do it anyway." Tsarno turns to move further into the room, but pauses, saying back over his shoulder, "By the way, Jean found me. Left him with one of our tech guys. Nice work on that map thing."

I start to get my warm, fuzzy, gloat-y feeling on, but before I can melt, another patron needs a drink. And as Tsarno begins taking his bulky self further into the mob, I see Inquistor Robur crossing the room. And although a good game player would be hustling up more patrons for more drinks, something about Inquistor Robur the Conqueror fascinates me and I keep watching. And then I begin to laugh; he's heading straight for, you guessed it, the well-exposed Ari. And as I watch, ignoring some festooned guy who wants to know if I have change and a wigged-out woman who wants a drink, craning my neck around some flame-throwing baton guy who momentarily blocks my view, something odd catches my attention.

With my head swiveling around and Ari looking up in conversation, it all kind of force perspectives my point of view, forcing my eyes almost directly behind Ari and meeting a different set of eyes. And this feeling that comes over me is not like one I've ever felt. I think it's what people call dread. The cold runs straight through my gut, up through my spine, and into my heart. My arm falls straight down, my hand still clenching the tray, but dropping the remaining few drinks onto the floor. "Um, Tsarnowsky?" I force the air up through my lungs. The voice barely squeaks. I am not sure if he heard my squeak or the drinks fall, but somehow through all the milling and din, something makes him stop and turn.

He comes back and I manage to lift my left hand and point, but he can't see it, he's not at the right angle. But I can't make my mouth move to form words to tell him. I can't tell him we were right but we were wrong and that we are too late. The statue, the one holding a good-sized, shiny round object, a shiny round object like a pearl . . . like a freaking pearl . . . isn't a statue at all. Or at least she hasn't been a statue. For long. We are so too late.

¤ ¤ ¤

Think, Sid. Think. My head spins. I try and hold it steady. Tsarno is yelling, barking orders. People are shrieking, seeing the police

143

rushing to a statue placed where she can watch the crowd, set proudly on a cement block, holding the pearl extended palm up as though an offering, and realizing it, she, is still, I don't know, not quite set, and it's too late.

I wonder if he is watching the madness. Getting off on it. If he's still here, I know the center stairs won't let him in unless he breaks through the whole librarian's area, which then actually would let him make his way down to the stacks underneath. If he gets down there, all bets are off. There are what, six or seven levels of stacks below and each one has theoretic exits . . . and a million zillion books. And Carnegie Steel shelving. And lots of exits. Which could explain Tessa and the Bryant Park connection. I mean maybe that was a dry run for this. Everyone knows the stacks run all the way underground from here to the Park. I glance over to the center square. Looks untouched.

Okay. That's not it. The dumbwaiter? No. Wouldn't fit a person. Keep thinking, Sid. The southwest stairs are too far away. There'd be no view and it's a long way to get to if you're in trouble. And that leaves the front entrance where I was standing or . . .

"It's the stairs!" I am screaming to Tsarno but he isn't there. Ari and Vikram are with me now. I don't know where he went or when they came. "He's using the northwest stairs into the stacks. It has to be. We need to tell Tsarno."

We look at each other and rush out into the hall. The staircases leading out are now mobbed. A police officer pushes a hand-cuffed, and now shockingly quite capable of screaming, Cannibal through the hall. Suddenly another crowd surge pushes from behind and Vik reaches out, grabs hold to steady me. The panic makes it nearly impossible to communicate anything. I manage to hang onto Ari for just a minute. "Get down there and find Tsarno or Emma or anybody, and tell them there's like a hundred ways out from in the stacks. They have to get down to the stacks."

Before they can argue, I pull out my phone and start pinging Jean wildly, hoping the pinging will get him to track my movements and tell someone to find me. And just as I take a deep breath, readying myself to swim upstream through the crowd and back to the northwest steps, I glance back over the rail. I see two police officers trying to escort people out the front doors at the same time I see Flynn and Imani fighting, pushing their way in. My eyes continue their sweep and I see a glint and I squint and the glint is a gun, like a real one and not a steampunked weapon and I don't stop, I scream and I don't think, I jump. And I fly.

And as I hear everyone shrieking, the clarinet player spins around from under me, twisting to his right in the process. I see him see me and smirk. He raises his clarinet and he shoots me. Oh my God, I've been shot by a clarinet! And it hurts. And I plummet.

Straight down to the hard, cold marble floor.

Whatever happened to the spiral of smoke?
There's always a spiral of smoke?

And . . .

. . . Crash.

But it is not the floor I hit. But I did hit something. Because I am very much alive and I am looking directly into the eyes of Detective Goddess Emma Macdonald, who ran and slid underneath me to break my fall . . . and save my life.

And Jimmy and Imani run over to me, screaming. Jimmy drops to the floor, his hands doing a dance in the air, but not knowing if they should touch me or not. I hear his, "Shit, Sid," and I try to look up. And although I can't quite get to "up," I can still see a small piece of Jimmy's face, enough to see the tears rolling down his cheek. I try to form my mouth into somewhat of a small smile. "Treppenwitz, Flynn, Treppenwitz."

TWENTY-FOUR

And there you have it. It may or may not have been what you were thinking, but I did make good on my promise to you. I did somehow manage to survive this act of immature-brain-encased-in-unbelievable-stupidity, and have now told you exactly how I got there.

So now, post having gotten there.

I was rushed by ambulance to the hospital, where not only did my friends race after me, but my parents were waiting. And once they ascertained I was not only very much alive, but declared not serious, nothing broken, just bruised, the night started to get very long. The gunshot wound was actually only a grazing of the back of my left leg, nothing a couple of bandages couldn't handle. I am expected to make a full and speedy recovery . . . at least, from my wounds.

However, being deemed "not seriously injured" in the emergency room moves you to the back of the line, leaving way too much time for parental bouts of crying from not only my parents, but Jimmy's parents, Imani's parents, and Vikram's father, who have by now all arrived, and are taking turns screaming and pleading, asking us over and over the dueling oxymoronic questions of the year "what were we thinking?" and "how could we?" It's been a kind of terrifying few hours.

And for me, it only got worse. At least we could take comfort in our numbers, but as the hours ticked by, each parent seemed to run out of expressible rage and thus claimed their child, who was inevitably dragged out looking helplessly back at me, leaving me alone as it grew later and I grew more tired and more scared. Without all the adrenaline, chills kicked in. But if I thought stoically listening and repeatedly apologizing would help this just blow over, or at least generate sympathy, that dream was shattered when my Dad calmly looked me in the eye and announced we would deal with this "once we got home."

By that time, I was closing my eyes to hide the eye roll and kind of hoping the hospital would change its mind and let me stay overnight. No such luck.

And I am apparently never going to have anything else to do because I am grounded for the rest of my life. Even my computer has been relocated from my bedroom. And while Jean is not grounded for life, his computer is currently at the table across from mine and he cannot go out on Friday and Saturday nights for the next month, which I don't think is really any hardship for him. I actually think he is the happiest I've ever seen him. Even though we didn't need to use Marauder's, he did it. And if I'd chased the guy into the stacks, he did have my back. So, I have to say, he was pretty impressive there for just a moment. Sadly, I don't think impressive is the word my parents will ever use for our exploits.

But speaking of our exploits . . .

It turns out we were more lucky in some ways than right. Detective Tsarnowsky came by with a Lieutenant Raymond P. Clark, apparently his boss, and they sat with me and my parents, sharing some of what they had learned.

The mastermind behind all of this was a twenty-eight year old shipping heir named Yanni Stanolopous. And when he was young, he was classified as intellectually gifted, but socially not so much. And his most favorite book, and his bestest—and only—friend, was Jules Verne's *Twenty Thousand Leagues Under the Sea*. And Yanni's father promised him when he grew up, he would build Yanni his very own Nautilus.

And it might have been just a boyhood dream except Yanni grew more and more obsessed, and by the time he was seventeen, the genius boy was a man caught in the early stages of schizophrenia. And with his family's money came a desire, and an ability, to try to manage this from Yanni's own apartment on Central Park West. And for Yanni, this was perfect. He needed everything kept secret because if the voices were found out, "they," his parents, doctors, etc., would try and stop him from his purpose. As the quote he had meticulously painted across his bedroom wall said, "I am not what you would call a civilized being! I have broken with society for reasons which I alone have the right to appreciate. So I do not obey its rules, and I ask you to never invoke them in my presence again." Chapter 1 *in 20,000 Leagues Under the Sea*. I'm definitely thinking he wasn't who Jules Verne had in mind.

And somehow this led, in ways way beyond my understanding, to throwing LARPs so he could fulfill his said purpose, which has something to do with killing three different someones in the manner in which they apparently deserved to die, and thus avenge the death of his ancestors at the hands of the British Raj in the Fourth Anglo-Mysore War.

And somehow by surveying his guests, he can find this person. Because you see, steampunk is very discerning. If you do not punk true, you reveal yourself to him. And it is okay, because this is his mission. "He is the law, and he is the judge!"

And like Captain Nemo, once he finishes taking care of this business, and his father rewards him with the promised Nautilus, which he knows his father is keeping from him until his quest is done, he will submerge and travel the waters forever.

And because no murder tale is complete without one ridiculously shocking plot twist, I present ours: It turns out Inquisitor Cyrus Porteus Stamford Robur was actually one Cyrus Frank Harding, a man hired by Yanni's father to be Yanni's caregiver, who instead got caught up in Yanni's quest, becoming . . . drumroll please . . . yes, you guessed it, Yanni's First Follower. And that my friends, *that* is the plot twist I never saw coming. I mean think about it. If Yanni's father had hired anyone else, anyone with a name other than Cyrus Harding, would any of this ever have happened?

Because, for those of you less fanatical about Jules Verne, Cyrus Harding just happens to be Captain Nemo's engineer from *The Mysterious Island*. An engineer versed in physics, chemistry and navigation, critical to the establishment of a mini-civilization in absolute isolation.

So now armed with a first follower, and an intense understanding of the dark web, Yanni set sail in a sea where none of his other minders could ever check his history or search his email and chart a course for just how deranged he had become. In the world of the web, he was Nemo; he was no one. It was perfect. Wow.

Needless to say, the police experts are still trying to piece it all together.

The live-events company, for example, was hired through the web, and they took care of hiring everyone else per Yanni's directions. So when the police interviewed them, they truly didn't know anything. Just that Yanni had brought in this covered block, which they would need to maneuver into place upstairs when he was ready. That it was some art thing to be unveiled. Until that night, everything was taken care of online. Tsarno paused, shook his head, "Party cost him a hundred grand to throw." I could hear my parents gasp. Tsarno did that kind of sardonic chuckle/shrug thing. "He charged it."

And, he also told us that while Emma and I were lying in state on the floor, here's what happened. Yanni did head for the stacks, but they had stationed officers underground at various points, including exits to the streets. Yanni ran down, probably to exit out to the street through the center staff door on level six, maybe heard a commotion from the officers, maybe just guessed right, but he turned, changed his plans and fled directly to the third level where he made his escape through Room 121, funny enough, the History Reading Room and from there, he ducked back into the crowd of Astor Hall fighting their way to the exit.

Tsarno asks me the question I still can't answer myself, "How'd I know it was him?"

"I don't know really." This is the part I hate. I wish I had a moment of sheer insight and brilliance to share, but the truth is I don't. I just keep seeing her eyeballs when I try and think it out. They were like marbles popping out from a statue. I wonder why he did that. "I know I saw a gun glint but according to the therapist I am now busy seeing," pause and make a face at mom, even though honestly it is kind of helpful to speak with someone who can't kick me out of school or something for a choice they don't approve of. "According to her, I apparently am suffering from Denialism and thus, I think I couldn't process that. So in my conscious head I thought, look at that guy with the clarinet. But that didn't make sense. Because there was no clarinet player. And Nemo was an organ player, but I didn't remember hearing an organ. So consciously I saw a clarinet, but in my unconscious head, I guess I knew it was a gun. And he was pointing it." I feel my panic start to rise. I don't like this part. "And he was waving it around, at the door, where Jimmy and Imani were coming in. I don't know if he would have shot the gun, but once I saw it, I just had to stop him." And I think to myself, and he had crazy eyes. And it was all about the eyes for just that minute.

But I don't say that out loud because as I said, it was better to be lucky than right. Given all the booze and the drugs and the chaos, in hindsight, I'd be willing to bet Yanni wasn't the only one with a gun, or crazy eyes. I could have killed myself and had nothing to show for it.

And suddenly I'm shaking and mom is holding onto me. But as much as I want to burrow into her, I can't. I'm not done. "And?" I needed to know. "The girl?"

Her name is, or was, or she was, but her name still is, Anushka Rao. She was in her second year of medical school. I think it's important for us, and you, to know this. We were right about his victims being part of the LARP; we were just wrong in how he chose them. Anushka was just the first person to arrive. Cyrus brought her in. Yanni didn't "circle the crowd" or anything, in order to actually pick her; she was just the first one there. And thus, she became the woman to offer up the giant pearl. And in his mind, as Cyrus brought her into him, that translated to fitting his criteria. But like Tessa, and like, if the circumstances were different and we just showed up early so we could cosplay, we probably would have volunteered. Remember, she came there to play her part, willing to die, for her art. Because who would ever have thought this would somehow be real?

And I guess because we really couldn't think that, we couldn't be early and save the day, or Anushka.

And with that truly sad, hard thought, the two officers stood, getting ready to go. The lieutenant shook both my parents' hands and then, when he got to me, he gave a little speech about how we shouldn't have been there, but still, how much they appreciated our assistance with some of our more specialized knowledge. It was a nice try. And I know Tsarno must have put him up to it.

And while that's the end of the more gruesome details, that's not quite the end of the saga. I mean I could tell you we're done; it's a pretty powerful ending, lots of food for thought in it, and you'd probably accept that.

Or we could talk about Tsarno stopping by again to check on me, say thanks—again, and apologize profusely to my parents—again, and you'd probably nod and say, nice of him or something less kind, depending on how culpable you think he is.

I mean, I don't think he's culpable. We do make our own stupid teenage brain choices, but why debate? It doesn't really matter. I'm just stalling. I would digress rather than stall, but I can't even think of a good digression. And you, you who have traveled so far with me, deserve only my best.

So instead, let's move on. Jimmy, Imani and Vik have also been deemed grounded-for-life, other than Jimmy gets mini-reprieves for football practice and games. At least he gets fresh air. However, he and Imani are currently rather annoyed with me, because it seems I am to blame, naturally, for their predicament, as though they had nothing to do with it, although I do give them both my sympathy and my empathy. Dating should be a one-on-one, full contact game and not some sort of weird writing competition with your work being closely supervised by your parents. I do remind them, grounding will end.

Ari, of course, managed to convince her parents none of it was her idea, which in fairness was kind of true and if they grounded her, she pointed out, she couldn't come study with me in an effort to boost her SAT scores and and and. So, she is not grounded for life, or even the weekend. One day I am going to get that girl to give me lessons, spin lessons.

And now, I guess it is time for me to bite the bullet, okay probably a poor choice of words given the circumstances, and cop to the rest. Great, I'll take that cliché, add one bad pun, and top it all off with one poor choice. Yep. I am just one big bouncing bundle of blab. So, let's just cut to the chase.

I was rushed to the hospital in a shared ambulance. My traveling companion was Detective Goddess Emma Macdonald. It seems, when she broke my fall, I broke her pelvis

So I go see her in the hospital. She saved my life. Even my parents couldn't say no to that request.

I ask her if she's okay. She laughs a little, asks if I'm okay. I sit down in the room's visitor chair. Then comes the silence. Awkward. I am not good with the whole silence thing. But not to worry, it's Suave Sid rushing to my rescue. "You know, this whole thing reminds me of this quote from *Finnegans Wake*."

"Sid," Emma gently cuts in, mercifully saving us both. "Come here."

I get up and move over toward the bed where she is motioning. She motions me closer and closer as though she has something private to say, but as I lean over, she grabs my shirt, pulls me down, and gives me a very soft, very gentle kiss. OMG! On the cheek, people! "Go. Go out there and find yourself a girlfriend before we all have to kill you."

And leaving the room, I think I should feel sad, but I don't. You know what, it's okay. I'm okay. Because, if we're being honest, after you break the pelvis of the woman of your dreams, the fantasy is never quite the same.

And I walk out the hospital's front door and I hear, "Need a ride?" I'd know that voice anywhere. It's Tsarnowsky, leaning his big old self against his beater car. Coincidence? Probably not.

"Nah." I look up at him and smile. "The faster I get home, the faster I must make my return to forced shut-in status." I pull my messenger bag around. "But thanks." I pull my sunglasses out, and turn away. It's time for Sid the Kid to ride off into her sunset, or at least, climb up to her High Line. Make her way home. Before it gets dark.

Acknowledgments

You can argue books are written in a vacuum, but you cannot argue they are published with the help of a whirlwind of Friends, Romans and Country-peeps ... who leant me way more than just their ears. And I do confess to having bent every one of them along this way!

First and foremost, you can't write smarter than you truly are without significant help. Neil Shaw—thank you for not just being a friend in need, but a geek indeed. Fay Jacobs—thank you for keeping my "brilliant" ideas supported, or in check, based upon whichever seemed a "more-better" outcome in the moment. You are the best friend and sounding board ever! Amanda June Hagarty—thank you for making me, and my profile, way savvier than we are.

So many friends who made time to read, give feedback, answer a question, make an introduction and sometimes just remember to ask how it's coming along without sounding "expectational"—THANK YOU. David Ray, Elizabeth Sims, Charles Ardai, Wendy Fishman, Jane McGregor, Candy Walters, Ileen Maisel, Shamim Sarif, Hanan Kattan, Ally Lattman, Eric Peterson, Elizabeth Coit, Caroline Stites, Bonnie Quesenberry, Lee Rose, Brenda Abell, Gregory Murphy, Michael Boyle, Cara Chaiet Morris, Jesikah Sundin, Russell Kolody, Sean Jaffe,

Lisa Rojany Buccieri, my "brothers in crime" Lloyd Segan and Shawn Piller and my super talented brother-in-law David Perl—love you all.

Ann McMan, thank you for designing a cover so perfect even I did not have a note to give. If you'd asked me what I wanted, I wouldn't have known the answer. To open your email and know it's exactly what I wanted—how delicious is that!

Bywater Books. Salem West. There is nowhere else professionally nor personally I would rather be.

To Elizabeth Andersen and Nancy Squires thank you for proper punctuation, attribution and spelling in other words, thank you for making me (and Sid) look 'literately' good.

To Alan Winnikoff and the entire team at Sayles & Winnikoff, thank you for believing Sid deserves her own headline!

To my family: Bernice-Cara-David-Jake-Andie-Evan-Joan-Hannah-Maddie-Kathleen-Shannon-Lori-Mark-Josh-Eric-Sheri-Emily-Madison . . . and Neal. Wow. I am blessed.

And for my partner, Nancy Prescott.

Thank you for loving me . . . and all my peeps who live inside . . .

. . . A Writer is a World Trapped in a Person

—Victor Hugo

About the Author

Television producer and writer Stefani Deoul is the author of the award-winning novel *The Carousel* and Supervising Producer of the television series *Haven* for the SyFy Network. Stefani has written for numerous publications, including, Curve magazine, Outdoor Delaware and Letters from CAMP Rehoboth, penned both short stories and film and television treatments and has produced TV series such as *The Dead Zone* and *Brave New Girl* along with being the executive in charge of production for the series *Dresden Files* and *Missing*.

The Carousel was a finalist for the Foreword Reviews Independent Publishing Award in Gay and Lesbian Fiction, won Fiction Book of the Year from the Delaware Press Association and was the Bronze winner in Fiction from the National Federation of Press Women. *The Carousel* also won a regional IPPY award in fiction from the Independent Publishers Association.

Along with producing five seasons of *Haven*, based on the Stephen King story *The Colorado Kid*, Stefani finally succumbed to the allure of acting, "starring" as the off camera, and uncredited, radio dispatcher, Laverne. When not filming, she now calls Sarasota, Florida home (even though Rehoboth Beach, a few Canadian Provinces and the Great White Way continue to inhabit special places in her heart), and is currently working on a new adventure for Sid and her friends.